THE WHITELANDS AFFAIR

By Anna Clarke

THE WHITELANDS
AFFAIR

ANNA CLARKE

A CRIME CLUB BOOK
Doubleday
NEW YORK   LONDON   TORONTO   SYDNEY   AUCKLAND

A Crime Club Book
Published by Doubleday, a division of
Bantam Doubleday Dell Publishing Group, Inc.
666 Fifth Avenue, New York, New York 10103

Doubleday and the portrayal of a man
with a gun are trademarks of
Doubleday, a division of Bantam Doubleday Dell
Publishing Group, Inc.

Library of Congress Cataloging-in-Publication Data

Clarke, Anna, 1919–
  The Whitelands affair.

  "A Crime Club book."
  I. Title.
PR6053.L3248W45   1989   823'.914   88-30019
ISBN 0-385-24984-5

THE WHITELANDS AFFAIR

1

The marmalade was very nearly ready to put into jars. Dr. Paula Glenning dipped a spoon into the simmering panful and dropped a little of the hot, sticky mixture onto a cold plate. It congealed at once, and she scooped it up with her finger and put it into her mouth.

"Lovely. Just right," she said aloud.

The telephone rang. She swore quietly, shifted the pan off the hotplate, picked up a ladle, and tried to ignore the ringing.

It was hopeless. Her task needed a steady hand, and the sense of urgency generated by the telephone bell unsettled her. She put down the ladle, wiped her sticky fingers on a damp cloth, and went into the living-room to pick up the receiver.

"I thought you were never going to answer," said James Goff reproachfully.

"I'm making marmalade. Can I call you back?"

"Well, it is rather urgent, and I've got to go out. I didn't know you ever made marmalade. Why have you suddenly become domesticated?"

"Why shouldn't I make marmalade? It's my grandmother's recipe. And it's going to spoil if I leave it much longer."

"You've never offered me any." The voice became more and more reproachful. "And I love home-made marmalade."

"Okay, you can have a jar," said Paula resignedly. "Do hurry up. What's so urgent?"

"William Burden. I'm going to lunch with him tomorrow, and he particularly wanted you to come along too."

"Why?"

"I think he's having marriage problems again," replied James cautiously.

"And what am I supposed to do about it? Anyway, he only got married again last year."

"Yes, that's the trouble. I mean, the ego and the public image can just survive having one wife run away, but they can't survive a repeat performance. My grandpa knew all about that. He took the precaution of acquiring a second wife who was completely dependent on him."

"All right, I'll come," said Paula. Her mind was still very much in the kitchen, and the quickest way to get back there was obviously to agree. "What time?"

"I'll call for you about half past ten."

"Isn't that awfully early?"

"There's something I need to do on the way."

If it hadn't been for the marmalade, Paula would have continued to protest, but as it was, she simply said, "I'll be ready. Goodbye, James."

He was still talking when she put down the telephone and ran back to the kitchen. The interruption had done no damage to the marmalade, but it had changed the nature of Paula's train of thought. Previously she had been in a vaguely nostalgic mood, remembering the grandparents who had brought her up and the market garden where she had spent her early childhood.

Now her thoughts turned to William Burden, recently retired professor of political economy. She had spoken to him once after a lecture he had given at the Princess Elizabeth College, where she taught, and once again at a college reception, but these very brief encounters had not aroused in her any desire to get to know him better. Her impression at the time had been of a rather conventional, very self-satisfied character, concealing his dislike of women academics under an exaggerated politeness.

James talked of him now and then, and they were obviously on friendly terms, which puzzled Paula until she discovered that

Professor Burden was considered to be very knowledgeable about stock-market movements.

Money. That explained a lot. Of course, James would act friendly towards somebody who gave good investment advice, but surely it need not extend to getting involved in a marriage breakdown? Paula thought not, and when James came to call for her the following morning, she told him so.

"Friends are friends," he replied rather irritably. "You can't make use of people when it suits you and fade away when they're in difficulties."

As this was just the sort of thing that James was sometimes inclined to do, Paula thought it wisest not to comment.

"What's the matter with Kitty Burden?" she asked instead.

"Good question. That's what you and I are supposed to be about to discover."

Paula groaned. "What a horrible prospect! Why on earth did you drag us into this? We're getting much too old to enjoy public discussion of personal relationships."

"I know. I'm sorry. I'm not looking forward to it either. Bloody impudence."

This last remark was addressed to the driver of a Rolls that had slipped past them into the faster lane in Piccadilly. James had recently exchanged his Land-Rover for a small Renault, much more convenient in London traffic, and his attitude towards other road-users seemed to be changing accordingly.

Paula sympathised, and the slight tension that had arisen between them eased off, only to return a minute later when she asked, "What are we doing in Piccadilly anyway? I thought they lived in Chelsea."

"Told you I'd got to go this way," muttered James.

"You said you'd got an errand. What is it?" demanded Paula.

James made no reply. He was very much occupied in getting round Hyde Park Corner, where vehicles were coming from all directions at once, and Paula, who always avoided driving here herself, did not repeat the question.

It had snowed again in the night, but you had to look far into the park to get any sense of true whiteness. The frozen heaps along the railings already looked more like lava than snow, and the pavements were deep in soft grey mud.

"Wouldn't it be nice," said Paula dreamily, "if we were just about to get on a plane for Tenerife. Or even if we were going to have another look at the Chagall exhibition and then lunch at the Festival Hall before the concert."

James sighed. "It would be very nice indeed. I'm going to have to confess. Would you mind waiting, love, until we get onto the A23?"

The Brighton road, said Paula to herself. If it had not been so obvious that James was feeling just as reluctant about this engagement as she was, she would have been even more annoyed with him. Curiosity, always a very strong motive in Paula, began to struggle with resentment and finally conquered.

"Tell me now," she said as they came over Vauxhall Bridge, "and I'll try to forgive you."

"The Burdens moved out of London a few months ago," said James.

"And where are they now?"

"At a village called Whitelands, just outside Brighton."

"Whitelands," repeated Paula. "Sounds kind of suburban."

"I don't know what it is," said James, relieved that she was taking it so calmly. "I've never been there, but I checked the route. It shouldn't take us much over an hour. Well, maybe a bit longer in this weather."

"Definitely a bit longer," said Paula, who did not enjoy fast driving in any weather. "I've got an idea," she added a moment later. "If it starts snowing again, and even if it doesn't, don't let's come back tonight. Why don't we find somewhere to stay in Brighton and go and build a snowman on the beach?"

"Anything you like. Once we are clear of our Burdens, the choice is yours. It's the least I can do for dragging you into this, but I couldn't face it without you. Am I forgiven?"

It was a rhetorical question. James knew that he would always be forgiven. Or, to put it another way, that he would never do anything completely unforgivable. And after all, thought Paula, it is usually the other way round nowadays: not James dragging me into other people's problems, but me dragging him.

"Why is William Burden afraid of losing another wife?" she asked.

James replied indirectly. "The trouble with Bill is that he has never quite made it to the top and will certainly never get there now."

"He's got an impressive list of publications in Who's Who."

"They're entirely derivative. Expounding somebody else's theories. He's never done anything original. Okay, so you're going to say that very few academics ever do, but—"

"I wasn't," interrupted Paula, "and I don't know anything about economics at all. Have you read anything of his, James?"

"Of course I haven't. I'm only giving the general opinion— which happens to coincide with his own opinion of himself, I suspect. He's a disappointed man. All this business of retiring early so that he can write his magnum opus—that's just a public relations act. I doubt if he'll ever write anything again, except maybe the odd book review."

"Chat shows? Instant expert opinion for the news bulletins?"

"Oh, he can do that sort of thing. He's got the right sort of appearance, and he makes all the correct noises. But for a man who had hoped to leave a mark in his own field of scholarship and to get his knighthood—"

For the next few minutes a traffic diversion demanded all James's attention and Paula digested what had been said.

"So the job of boosting Bill's ego falls on his wife," she said presently.

"Exactly."

"And she's wishing she hadn't taken it on?"

"That is the question. Kitty is more than twenty years younger than he is. She was his secretary. Very devoted and admiring. Supported him when Greta ran off with the milkman."

Paula knew this last statement to be an exaggeration. The first Mrs. Burden had actually gone to live with a dairy farmer in the Welsh mountains.

"It all looked very satisfactory," continued James. "A totally loyal wife for Bill for the rest of his life, used to all his little ways, knowledgeable about his work, might even prod him into producing something worthwhile."

"And for Kitty?"

"A big jump up the social scale, a nice comfortable home, and the prospect of a prosperous widowhood."

"Is he in bad health?"

"Not that I know of."

"Then Kitty might have twenty years to wait. The best years of her life. That's an awfully long time if she's— How old did you say she was, James? Fortyish?"

"Thereabouts."

"Same age as you and me," said Paula.

The village of Whitelands was further from Brighton than they had expected. It was tucked away in a fold of the hills, the only access being along a winding lane. On either side were high banks from which the snow was sliding to add to the deep slush already in the roadway.

"I hope we don't meet anything," said Paula a trifle anxiously.

She always felt uneasy in narrow, shut-in places and was beginning to have the sensation of going round in circles.

"I can see the church tower," said James. "And look, the sun's coming out."

It was only a hazy sunshine, but it lifted the spirits and gave a faint sparkle to the untouched white of the hills and fields.

They drove past a petrol service station, a couple of shops, an inn, and some not very interesting stone cottages.

"He said next to the church," said James, stopping at the entrance of the large and crowded graveyard that dominated the tiny flint church at its centre and, indeed, the whole village.

"They certainly don't believe in keeping death out of sight," remarked Paula as she got out of the car. "It's a nice church though." She walked under the lych-gate. "Looks pre-Norman. Round tower, those little slits of windows—"

"Lots of ancient churches in Sussex." James joined her. "That's a useful topic of conversation if we run dry or if things look like getting awkward."

"Look at those yew-trees. And the size of those tombstones." She bent over to read from one of them: " 'Emilia Alexandra, Devoted Wife and Mother.' How would you like to be remembered as a devoted husband and father, darling?"

"I wouldn't mind the husband part. Do come away, Paula. We're supposed to be lunching with the Burdens. Their house is called The Twitten. This must be it."

"You can't call a house a twitten," objected Paula. "It's a local name for a narrow passageway."

"I know, and there it is. Flint walls either side. Hi, Bill! We've made it."

The man who was coming towards them was of medium height and was wearing light blue trousers and a chunky navy blue fisherman's jersey. To Paula, who had met Professor William Burden only on formal occasions, he looked the reverse of casual. He would have done very well, she thought, as a model for holiday wear for the over-sixties.

The thick grey hair, the sudden lighting up of the face in welcome, the outstretched hand, all belonged to the image.

The hand was held out to Paula, but the words were addressed to James.

"So you've brought her along." And then, as if hastily recollecting himself, he turned to her: "I hope you didn't have too bad a drive. It's very kind of you to come. Kitty will be delighted. She'll join us shortly. I believe she is at rather a critical stage in the kitchen."

They followed him through the pretty wrought-iron gateway set in the wall and along a garden path lined with rose-trees and neat piles of snow.

The Twitten was a square, solid-looking house that had probably been there for several centuries, although the flint walls were so hard and had weathered so well that they did not give the appearance of age.

"There's a cloakroom here," said William Burden, indicating a door to the right of the entrance hall, "and then if you'd like to join us for a drink—"

"The perfect host," muttered Paula to James when they were alone for a moment. "He's even worse than I remember. Terribly anti-woman."

"Oh, come, come," said James, glancing at himself in the mirror, "he's hardly spoken yet."

"I'm to be treated as a mere appendage to you," grumbled Paula as she washed her hands. "Kitty is to be discovered where the wife rightly belongs—in the kitchen."

"Aren't you being the teeniest bit touchy, darling?"

"It's you who dragged us into this," snapped Paula. "And I thought that was why we were here—to boost the morale of the wife. Or are we really here to beat her down further? Come on, James. Confess."

"I don't know. Honestly I don't. Bill phoned me and said he was worried about Kitty. He thought she might be getting rather bored and needing some stimulating society. He never actually *said* he was afraid she might up and off like Greta—that was me reading between the lines."

"Did he actually ask you to bring me?" demanded Paula.

"Well, sort of. No. All right, then. He didn't suggest it straight away. It was only when he thought I might not accept that he suggested I should bring my . . . my friend. Actually I didn't feel that I could face it without you."

"Then take care, mate. Don't you dare start ganging up with Bill against us. None of this subtle or not so subtle anti-woman stuff. And for heaven's sake, James, darling James, don't let us get ragged into discussing our own relationship—you and me. Promise."

"Promise. Cross my heart."

"Then let's go."

"It sounds," said James as they returned to the hall, "as if there are other guests. That ought to help."

The sound of voices came from a large corner room that had one set of windows looking out down the main street of the village and another giving a view across snowy fields and distant hills.

Bookcases lined the inner walls; there were plenty of comfortable chairs, a log fire was burning on the hearth, and a big black-and-white cat got up from the hearthrug as they entered and insisted on being made a fuss of by James.

He bent down to oblige, while Paula surveyed the human occupants of the room. Apart from William Burden, there were two of them, introduced as Louise and Henry Graverton.

The telephone rang as the introductions were being made, and Bill excused himself.

"I'll take it in the study. Help yourselves to drinks."

He waved a hand towards the table that stood to the left of the fireplace.

Henry Graverton, a tall grey-haired man wearing large spectacles and a rather shabby tweed suit, took over without any fuss. Louise, who looked younger than her husband, handed glasses to Paula and James.

"Graverton," said Paula as they all settled on chairs near the fire and the cat jumped up onto James's knee, "the name reminds me of algebra lessons."

"That's us," said Henry and Louise with one voice.

"Or rather," added Louise on her own, "it's been a joint effort for the past twenty years, since Henry and I married. The books you used at school were probably Henry's own efforts."

She smiled at Paula. She was as tall and thin as her husband

and had a narrow face surrounded by thick black hair. Paula felt
at home with her at once.

"I can't believe I'm meeting Graverton's maths textbooks,"
she said. "It's rather like being introduced to the Albert Memorial. Don't you think so, James?"

"I'm sorry to say," said James, "that I never had the benefit of
Graverton. But that's because I never had the benefit of a proper
education. I was at one of the Great English Public Schools," he
explained with mock solemnity to Henry and Louise.

Conversation became general, friendly, and animated.

"Have you come down from London too?" asked James.

"No. We live here."

It seemed that the Gravertons had a habit of speaking in uni-
son.

"In Whitelands?"

"Yes. Why not?" It was Henry who answered. "I retired from
teaching a couple of years ago, and Louise goes into Brighton
twice a week to take remedial maths classes."

"No more textbooks?" asked James.

"Only a little guide for computing beginners. Louise bullied
me into it because she says that otherwise she'd never see me."

"Plants and birds," explained his wife. "Henry has been a
frustrated naturalist all his life, and he now spends his days
searching for different species." Turning to Paula, she added,
"I'm so glad it isn't bugs or spiders. It's bad enough finding a
glass jar full of poisonous-looking berries in the fridge, but if it
were a black furry, leggy corpse . . ."

Professor Burden returned to the room.

"Getting to know each other?" he said. "That's fine."

But actually his arrival broke up the pleasantly relaxed atmosphere, and everybody seemed to become a little tense.

"That was the vicar," he explained. "He's coming in for a
drink and a chat later this afternoon. You'll stay, won't you?" he
went on, turning to James and Paula. "We were rather hoping to

persuade you to stay the night, now that the weather is worsening."

Paula looked at James in alarm, and then she looked out of the window and saw that it was snowing heavily again. The sensation of being trapped, which had eased during their conversation with Henry and Louise, returned in full force. James must not accept. She could not possibly stay in this house overnight. William Burden was one of those people who make the very air of a room feel oppressive. To sit through a meal and act politely for a couple of hours was the utmost she could achieve.

If James were to accept, then she must have an excuse to get away. Her mind worked frantically to find a reason why she had to leave.

"It's very kind of you," said James. "Actually we weren't proposing to drive back to London tonight, but we've fixed to visit some people in Brighton. Connected with Sussex University. It seemed a good opportunity."

Paula feared that her relief must be obvious to everybody in the room. It was not the first time she had felt grateful to James for being so fluent a liar, but she could not help wondering what he would say if Bill Burden asked who those people were. Probably James would throw it over to her. She thought for a moment and remembered a former student of hers who was working for a higher degree at Sussex. That would have to do.

Fortunately Bill did not enquire. Paula began to relax, but she had been shaken by the irrational panic that had overwhelmed her when Bill gave his invitation, and was afraid that it could return. Get a grip on yourself, she told herself firmly. You're only here as a guest, an observer. You're not his wife; you're not trapped here. They are not even your friends: they are friends of James's.

The thought of James brought with it a resentment that undid all her struggle for composure. It was mean of him to trick her into coming here. But it was also her own fault. She ought to have told him to drive her to the nearest South London tube

station and gone straight home when she found that they were
not going to Chelsea. What they needed now, she and James,
was to be alone together so that they could sort it out between
them, quarrel a bit, sulk a bit, and restore their goodwill.

Instead of which they were condemned to be witnesses to a far
less happy and loving relationship than their own. It was going
to be horrible. They were going to be treated like the unfortunate visiting couple in *Who's Afraid of Virginia Woolf.*

Henry Graverton was talking about the new bird table that he
had set up in his garden. "If this weather keeps on, we might get
some unusual visitors," he said. "We've had a couple of red-
wings come to feed this morning."

Paula dredged up a memory of her early childhood. "Did
they actually come to the table," she asked, "or did they feed on
the ground, like the thrushes?"

"To the table," replied Henry, "but very nervously."

"It always surprises me," remarked James, "when Paula pro-
duces a piece of country lore. For me, she's the essential Londoner."

"I used to be that too," put in Louise, "but I've really come to
like living here."

Bill Burden, plainly discomposed at being left out of this conversation, embarked on a long description of the bird visitors to
his own garden that continued until their hostess appeared at the
door, apologising for not having greeted them earlier and an-
nouncing that lunch was ready.

2

Paula had formed a mental image of Kitty Burden, the secretary-turned-wife. Efficient, tactful, neat, unobtrusive, not plain but not too good-looking, mindful of everyone's comfort, and ready at any moment to throw a flattering light upon her husband.

If that was the role that Kitty had assigned herself, no wonder that the marriage was already beginning to crack. Twenty years or even more—for Bill Burden looked as if he might live till ninety—was a very long time indeed to play the part of such a paragon.

All these speculations and preconceptions were scattered to the winds by the appearance of Kitty herself. She was lovely to look at, with a sleek, 1920s type of prettiness, accentuated by her hair style and the plain light blue dress that she wore.

Paula looked at her with envy, not for the beauty, since she had never felt dissatisfied with her own modest share, but for her ability to produce a meal for six people and still look as if she had stepped out of a fashion-plate. She glanced at Louise Graverton as they filed out of the room, wondering if she was feeling the same, but Louise and Henry were keeping close together and taking no notice of anybody else, and Paula felt a momentary stab of envy of them too: they seemed to be a genuinely happy couple.

Her mood was not improved when they came into the dining-room and Kitty Burden, with a most inviting smile, ordered James to sit next to her. Had they met before? Paula could not remember. Possibly James had mentioned Kitty, but she had not been paying much attention. Paula herself was seated the other side of the table, between Bill Burden and Henry Graverton and opposite Louise.

Bill served goulash from the big pottery dish in front of him, and the guests were instructed to help themselves to baked potatoes and salads. Paula's normally healthy appetite had almost completely disappeared. Resentment at being made use of nagged at her, and she was overwhelmed by an aching longing to be anywhere else in the world but here. It was only with a very great effort that she responded courteously to Bill's enquiries.

"Are you planning any further ventures into biography?"

He managed to make it sound as if her very successful study of James's eminent grandfather, the novelist G. E. Goff, was a trivial and amateurish piece of work.

"Not at the moment," she replied. "The teaching seems to be occupying all my energies."

"Ah, you poor things. Still on the treadmill. That's where we oldies benefit. Freedom from the daily grind, beautiful surroundings, the peace and quiet of the country—though, of course, there are so many calls on one's time . . ."

It occurred to Paula, in the midst of her own preoccupations, that Bill, too, was losing his grip of himself, and this was causing him to babble idiotically. At the other end of the table Kitty was listening to James with the most flattering attention, and James seemed to be enjoying it. I suppose he thinks he is doing detective work, thought Paula bitterly, investigating Kitty's state of mind. Presumably I am meant to be studying Bill's. Well, it doesn't need much study. He's wildly jealous, which is perfectly natural, but I can't stand the man and I'm not going to play the game. I can't stand it. I want out.

Had it been her own car standing outside the front gate, Paula would have disgraced herself by breaking all the rules of society. She could actually picture herself standing up and saying, "Excuse me, but I have to get back to London before the weather gets any worse. Goodbye." A quick dash to the cloakroom to collect her things, a few moments fighting off the shocked protestations, and then the enormous relief of freedom.

But James had the keys to the Renault.

How else could she escape? Pretend to be ill? The way she was feeling now, it wouldn't take much pretence. She was not far off the sort of claustrophobic panic that occasionally assailed her in an overcrowded lecture room or at some particularly stressful committee meeting.

She pushed aside her plate, having barely touched the food, and took a drink of wine. Henry Graverton, on her left, said something to her, and Paula turned and smiled at him without having taken in what he said. She drank some more wine. The shining chestnut-coloured wood of the table, the blue-and-white plates, the faces of the guests, the French impressionist prints on the walls, and the relentlessly falling white flakes behind the long window, all began to shift about and blend into each other.

Paula put down her wineglass but did not loosen her grip on the stem. The thin cylinder of glass felt like the one solid thing in a dissolving world. It was many years since she had had so bad an attack. She could make no more effort. She could only sit, sick, giddy, paralysed, until somebody came to the rescue.

It was Louise Graverton who brought release. Through gradually clearing mists Paula heard the calm, good-humoured voice with its faint Scottish accent.

"If you've got caught up in local activities, Bill, it's your own fault. I warned you not to let Henry grab you for his environmental group, but you wouldn't listen, and of course, once it became known that you could be persuaded to subscribe and actually serve on the committee—"

"Then all the rest of the do-gooders moved in," concluded Henry. "Louise is perfectly right. You ought to have shut yourself up in your study and got Kitty to guard you like a dragon."

"But it's Kitty who wanted me to take an active part in village affairs," said Bill plaintively.

Paula—now well on the way to recovery, for these attacks,

once broken, left no lasting effects—ate some bread roll and salad and listened attentively.

Bill sounded on the defensive, but there was an underlying complacency about him that made Paula suspect that he was pleased at the direction the conversation had taken. The guests were reacting as he had hoped; they were playing his game.

Was his wife going to play it too? All eyes were turned towards her: would she respond to her cue?

"Do I hear my name?"

Kitty turned away from James and looked straight down the table at her husband. She picked up her wineglass as she spoke but put it down again without drinking. She had beautiful hands, Paula noticed, and they were constantly in motion, crumbling bread, shifting her knife and fork around, twisting her table napkin. It was the only sign of nervousness that she displayed. Her face and her voice were very much under control.

"Is Bill on at his usual theme?" she said, glancing at each guest in turn and ending up by addressing Louise.

"I've been telling him it's his own fault," replied Louise. "And Henry's," she added as if as an afterthought.

"Don't drag me in," protested her husband. "I don't really expect anybody else to share my enthusiasms. Though, of course, I'm very pleased when they do. And to have Bill's support over that oil-drilling proposal—"

"Oil?" put in James. "Surely not oil in this neighbourhood."

"Yes, my boy, oil," said Bill cheerfully. "They're hunting for it in some of the loveliest countryside in Sussex."

James and Paula made suitably horrified noises and managed to exchange private glances of support and sympathy while all the others were talking with great animation. The possible environmental disaster proved to be a life-saver for the social occasion. Nothing welds people together more than joining forces against a common enemy, thought Paula.

And oil, it seemed, was not the only threat. There was also a road-improvement scheme which would swallow up large chunks of land belonging to somebody called Roger and would turn the little approach lane to the village into a kind of minimotorway.

Privately Paula thought this a very good idea and was pleased to hear James saying so openly.

"But you need a better road, Bill. How on earth do the delivery trucks get through? And what happens when the lane is blocked by snow?"

"Roger lets them use his farm road if the lane is impassable," was Bill's reply. "It's rather a rough track, but it's wider than the other. You could have come that way if you'd wanted to."

"But I didn't know about it. You never told me."

James sounded aggrieved, but Paula mentally applauded him. There was so much falsity at this lunch party that it came as a relief to hear James's bad temper. At least it was a genuine human reaction, and she felt encouraged enough to say, "What is the objection to a better road?"

"Tourists, of course," replied Bill in a contemptuous manner and with a lift of the eyebrows as if he was amazed at Paula's stupidity.

"But what is there for tourists to look at in Whitelands?" persisted Paula. She had quite got over her own fit of claustrophobia, and her natural curiosity was beginning to reassert itself. "I'd never even heard of the place until James said we were coming here, and I do happen to know this neighbourhood fairly well."

"The church," said Bill as if reading from a guidebook, "has several unique features. So does Boyds. That is Roger Aston's estate. A very old family, and an old and interesting manorhouse. And of course you realise that we are not very far from Charleston Farmhouse, the Vanessa Bell–Duncan Grant ménage, and Virginia Woolf is believed to have cycled along the bridlepath that leads past this house when she rode over from Rodmell to see her sister. These are the sort of literary associations that draw the American visitors. Of course, I have no knowledge of literature—a mere juggler with statistics, that's me. But I should have thought that you and James—"

"We've seen the Woolf house at Rodmell," said James, coming to Paula's rescue, "but for some reason or other we've never been to Charleston. At any rate, I haven't. Have you, Paula?"

Paula shook her head.

"Would it be open now?" asked James, glancing around the table and addressing nobody in particular.

It was Kitty who answered. "It's only open in summer, but it's well worth a visit. I've been several times. It always makes me feel envious. What lucky people they were, doing their own thing and leading their own sort of Bohemian life in the Sussex countryside and not caring what anybody thought of them. And plenty of money in the background. That must have been true freedom."

She was speaking as if to herself, staring at the bowl of fruit in front of her and seeming quite unaware of her surroundings. Paula noticed that for the first time during the meal her restless hands were still.

"What is it precisely that you envy?" asked Bill, staring straight at his wife. "Is it the artistic ability? Or is it the ménage à trois with the live-in lover and the complacent husband?"

There was a perceptible pause before he continued, but nobody spoke. We are powerless to prevent an explosion, thought Paula, who was still looking at Kitty's hands. One of them was now out of sight under the table; the other was holding on to the wineglass as if it were a lifeline, much as Paula herself had been doing not very many minutes ago.

"I'm afraid we cannot hope that you will ever acquire any artistic ability," went on Bill. "But the ménage à trois might be arranged, if that is what you wish. Perhaps you have already selected a candidate?"

Not knowing what she was doing, Paula got to her feet and spoke: "I can't and won't put up with this. I'm going."

Nobody took any notice of her. They were all looking at

Kitty, who remained silent and motionless for a moment or two after Bill had finished speaking, and then she got up and looked around at her guests with a vague, sweet smile before leaving the room, not having uttered a word.

Paula rushed after her and caught her up at the foot of the stairs.

"What are you playing at?" she demanded furiously. "We come a long drive in vile weather, only to have to listen to this! Why the hell can't you settle your domestic difficulties in private? What are James and I expected to do now? Take sides? Both on the same side? Or are you trying to make us miserable as well?"

"I didn't know you were coming," said Kitty in a very low voice. "I didn't invite you. Bill did."

"I don't believe you."

"It's true. I can't help what you believe. I don't care what you believe. It's nothing to do with you. Let me go, Paula. I've got to swallow some pills. I need some rest."

Paula eased her grip on Kitty's wrist. The matter-of-fact hopelessness of this last speech had been very convincing.

"I'm sorry," she said. "Is there anything I can do?"

"Not unless you want to come upstairs and hear a sob-story." Kitty smiled faintly. "Some women enjoy that sort of thing."

"I've heard too many of them, and I don't enjoy it," said Paula, finding herself unexpectedly beginning to warm to Kitty. "But it's probably less awful than the alternative of returning to the dining-room."

Kitty's smile became broader. "I think I can promise you that. Your charming James will have more to put up with than you."

"Serves him right," said Paula as they went upstairs side by side.

The house was even bigger than it had appeared from outside. As in many old houses, the upper staircases and corridors were rather narrow, but the bright wallpapers and plenty of wall lighting mitigated this fault, and the overall effect was cheerful and pleasing.

Paula remarked on this to Kitty.

"Oh yes, I did my best," said Kitty indifferently.

At the top of the second flight of stairs they came to a door leading into a small room overlooking the church.

"This is my haven," said Kitty.

The room was furnished as an office, with a wooden desk, typewriter, and filing cabinet. There was also a divan bed and an old but comfortable armchair.

"The contents of my London bed-sit," said Kitty. "Minus the kitchen and bath. This is how I used to live. I feel at home here. And I like the view."

Together they walked over to the window.

"Tombstones," said Paula.

"They put our little nonsenses into perspective, don't they?"

"They do indeed. And I like the inscriptions."

"Gorgeously hypocritical."

"Guilty, more likely. You've loathed somebody during life, so you try to make up for it after death."

"Attributing to them the virtues you wished they had had."

They smiled at each other.

"Smoke?" asked Kitty, turning to the desk and picking up the packet of cigarettes that lay there.

"Thanks."

"Tea?"

"Please."

Kitty switched on a kettle and produced tea-bags and two large blue-and-white-striped mugs from the bottom drawer of the desk.

"Did you always look so glamorous," asked Paula, "when you were working as his secretary?"

"No. Actually I was rather sloppy. Like you."

"Thanks."

They both laughed.

"This is nice," said Kitty, leaning back on the divan bed. "You're doing me good. I guess I'm going to get through without taking any pills."

"Personally I prefer nicotine to Valium," remarked Paula, "but it is less socially acceptable."

They smoked and drank in friendly silence for a little while. Then Kitty said, "The sob-story. Three sentences are enough. I have a severely mentally handicapped daughter who is well cared for in a private home. Bill agreed to pay the fees. The price was marriage."

Paula digested this.

"Sex?" she said presently.

"No problem. Bill has always been more interested in boys than in girls. And I have a friend whom I see frequently."

Paula wondered for a moment whether this "friend" was male or female, finally deciding that it was the former and that Bill knew about it and didn't care. His viciousness towards Kitty was much more complicated and less healthy than a straightforward sexual jealousy.

"So he provides the money, and your job is to—"

Paula paused expectantly.

"Keep up appearances," said Kitty. "That's all he wanted. That's all I bargained for. I've done my best to keep my side of the bargain."

"But he hasn't?"

Kitty shrugged and lit another cigarette. "Judge for yourself."

"Was this sort of . . ." Paula hesitated, unable to find the right words for Bill's behaviour at the lunch table. "What was the keeping up appearances intended to include?" she asked instead.

"Homemaker, housekeeper, and hostess," replied Kitty. "That's the easy part. I don't particularly like the job, but I don't like shorthand and typing either. It's a job. I think I do it well enough."

"You most certainly do," said Paula. "Surely he can't have any complaints on that score?"

"No. It's with the difficult part that I seem to be failing."

"You mean the ego-boosting?"

"That's right."

"But Kitty," said Paula earnestly, leaning forward in her armchair and dropping ash onto the carpet, "you'd worked as his secretary for years. You knew what he was like. You'd coped with it."

"Marriage is different. That's where I made the mistake. I should have held out for us just sharing a house and making it appear as if we were living together in every sense of the word."

"But he wanted the legal tie?"

"Yes. Not only because he thought it would be harder to break. He likes to be able to say 'my wife.' "

"It's odd," said Paula thoughtfully, "how men seem to have this need. It's never given me any sort of kick to be able to say 'my husband.' How about you?"

Kitty shook her head. "Means nothing to me. Your handsome James?" she added questioningly.

"He goes through a phase of it every now and then. I'm sure it would totally ruin our good relationship. I'm hopeless as a wife. I tried it once and made a rotten job of it. Kitty, do you want to talk about your daughter?"

"Marie. She's a severe case of Down's syndrome. They can do a lot for the lighter cases nowadays. That's why I kept on hoping. But she's eighteen now and she's not going to improve. On the contrary. Unfortunately the life expectancy is . . . is higher than it used to be."

Kitty coughed, stubbed out her cigarette, and took a drink of tea. "I reckoned I could stick it out with Bill until she died," she went on presently. "After that? Well, it wouldn't much matter. Maybe I'd break my side of the bargain. I don't know and I don't care."

Her bleak self-control was painful to watch. Paula, who had

been rather dreading an emotional outburst, almost began to wish that Kitty might break down.

"You'll want to know about Marie's father," went on Kitty in the same toneless voice. "We were fellow students at a business college; each of us had been an only child who didn't make friends easily. He wanted us to marry after Marie was born, but I didn't feel I could cope with two feeble creatures, even though we didn't know then how hopeless a case Marie was. I don't know what became of him. We lost touch completely. My parents helped me financially. I didn't know until after they died that they were doing this out of their capital and living on less and less themselves. That was two years ago. I didn't know where to look next for money, and I thought I was going to have to take Marie away from the home, where I feel happy about her, and put her in—"

For the first time Kitty's voice showed emotion, and Paula could hardly hear what she said.

"Marie doesn't really notice her surroundings all that much, but I notice them. All the time, whatever I am doing, I have a picture of her in my mind. So it's for my sake, not for hers. I am sure you think it absurd, perhaps even wrong, that other lives should be sacrificed in order to maintain a semi-vegetable child in comfort."

She leaned forward and looked straight at Paula, who found it very difficult to make an honest response, since her immediate reaction to the story had indeed been something of that sort.

"I wouldn't blame you," went on Kitty. "That's what everybody else thinks."

"Not exactly wrong," said Paula. "Certainly not absurd. I think mainly . . . just terribly sad. And I've no right to judge. I haven't any children, sick or well. It's your choice. You've a right to your own choice."

" 'Take what you want and pay for it, says God'?"

"Well, yes. But in your case there seems to have been a hell of a lot of paying and precious little taking."

Kitty made no reply, and they sat for a few minutes in silence. The little room felt quite detached from the rest of the house. Its atmosphere, thought Paula, was very much like that of her own attic room in Hampstead: very private, lacking in all pretence. She was about to ask Kitty how she managed to keep Bill out of it, when there was the sound of voices on the stairs.

"Kitty! Are you there?"

Henry and Louise were shouting together.

Paula swore; Kitty said that she was surprised that their peace had lasted so long.

"Coming!" she shouted back.

Louise was standing outside the door, somewhat out of breath and looking as if she was struggling to control her exasperation.

"Bill swears he has been poisoned. Please come and deal with him. Henry and I have got to go. The snow's worse than ever and he's worried about the chickens."

"I don't want to lose any more to the fox," said Henry rather more mildly, "and the last time it snowed—"

Kitty interrupted him. "Okay. I understand. You've had enough of us. Thanks for coming anyway. Where's Bill?"

"In the sitting-room."

Kitty ran downstairs.

"Is he really ill?" Paula asked Louise.

The Gravertons seemed quite willing to be detained, and Henry answered, "He gets attacks of indigestion sometimes. That's probably all it is."

"But why did you say 'poisoned'? We've had nothing to eat that could cause food poisoning." Paula looked from one guarded face to the other. "Please," she went on, addressing Louise, "if James and I are going to be left to cope with this, it would help to have your honest opinion. You know Bill and Kitty much better than we do."

After silently communicating with her husband, Louise said, "Our advice to you is to keep out of it. Don't take sides. I know it's not easy, but if you and James stick together—"

"How can we stick together?" demanded Paula. "I've chosen Kitty, and James is siding with Bill. He is, isn't he?"

She glanced at Henry, who said, "At the moment, he is agreeing with Bill that Kitty might have put something noxious in his salad, but he's probably only saying that to humour Bill."

"His salad! But we all ate the salad," exclaimed Paula.

"Bill had a separate bowl. Didn't you notice? He can't eat onion. It gives him violent indigestion."

"Then that explains it. He obviously took some out of the wrong bowl."

"I'm quite sure you are right," said Henry. "It's very easily done. But it's much too simple an explanation for the Burdens. They've got to have drama, and the more people to watch it, the better."

"So this isn't the first time?"

As she spoke, Paula stepped back into Kitty's little sanctum, and the others followed her. She felt guilty about the intrusion, particularly when Louise remarked that she had never been in there before, but she was determined not to let the Gravertons leave the house without getting some more information out of them.

Henry seemed more inclined to talk than his wife. Paula turned to him.

"Have you seen this sort of thing before—Bill accusing Kitty of trying to poison him?"

"Yes, we have. The worst occasion was only last week. We were having a meeting here to discuss the new road proposals."

"And we never got round to them at all," put in Louise.

She was standing just inside the door, and Paula noticed that she was looking round and taking in all the details of Kitty's room.

"No, we seldom talk much business when we meet at The Twitten," agreed Henry. "On that occasion there were about a dozen of us here. Roger Aston and his son, Philip. Bob Fulham —that's our vicar—and Glenys (sister, not wife), and the Reid family, who run the pottery-and-craft shop and whom I suspect are actually in favour of better communications for Whitelands, but they don't want to offend the nobs of the village. Kitty had produced her usual excellent sandwiches and cakes, and she was handing round some delicious-looking sugary morsels when Bill asked very loudly whether those were her rat-poison specials. You go on." Henry turned to Louise. "You're better at a story than I am."

Louise took up the tale a little reluctantly, Paula thought.

"Everybody laughed, but it wasn't really funny. There was too much venom in it. Bill went on to explain that he had come into the kitchen when Kitty was making the cakes, and he noticed that she had left items from her shopping on the other end of the kitchen table. Among them was a packet of rat-poison."

"How did Kitty react?" asked Paula.

"Very cool. Just ignored it. Bill went on and on, and we all got more and more uncomfortable. The only way to break it was for somebody to take one of the cakes, but everyone managed to avoid it, including Henry and myself, until it came to Glenys Fulham. She was probably the oldest person there—a rather quiet and self-effacing lady. She ate one of the cakes and said, 'Delicious, thank you, Kitty,' and after that Bill had to shut up."

Paula could picture the scene only too clearly.

"But what is he trying to do?" she asked. "If he goes on like this, they'll have no friends left. And they badly need friends."

The Gravertons looked at each other, yet again silently exchanging thoughts. Paula, who had liked them so much at first, began to feel irritated. If an unhappy couple made very poor company, a happy couple could be equally off-putting in its own way.

Henry answered at last, "It is not possible to be a friend to both of them. You choose one or the other, or else you keep out of it."

"And you've chosen to keep out of it?"

"We are certainly going to do our best."

"As you would too if you lived here," added Louise.

Paula felt their joint strength, resented it, and envied it. "I wish I could feel so detached," she said. "It must be a great asset."

Yet again the other two exchanged glances. "I suppose that it was inevitable you should choose Kitty," said Louise.

"And James choose Bill. And God knows what the two of them are going to do to James and me," said Paula. "Yet I can't help feeling for Kitty."

"Neither can we," said Louise. "We aren't completely heart-less, you know. Otherwise we wouldn't have come today. But never again. It's obvious that there is going to be no more at-tempt at a normal social life. Kitty doesn't confide in us, but she knows where we are, and she knows she can take refuge with us in an emergency."

"So you are on Kitty's side," said Paula, softening a little.

"She seems at the moment to be the greater sufferer," said Henry, "but I think it is probably Bill who is in greater need of a friend. Try not to take James away from him, Paula. For all your sakes. Forgive me if I sound interfering."

"You sound very wise," said Paula. "And I'm grateful. I'll go down now."

"And we are quietly going to disappear. Would you like our phone number?"

Paula noted it, feeling more and more guilty about her own little outburst against them.

On the stairs she said, "Louise— Henry— Do you think Bill has any reason to be afraid? Could Kitty really be planning to poison him?"

"That's exactly what we are wondering ourselves," replied the Gravertons almost with one voice.

3

There was no sign of life in the hall, and no sound came from behind any of the closed doors. While Henry and Louise were fetching their coats and boots, Paula went to the front door and looked out. The garden path had disappeared, and there was very little visible of the blue of James's Renault. A few yards down the village street, outside the shops, were signs of activity. Several cars were parked there, and a couple of human figures, too muffled up to be distinguishable as to sex, were carrying boxes of provisions and calling out to each other.

Further down the hill, in the near distance, Paula could see the tops of trucks and vans moving along the main road. Comforted by these signs of normal life in the outside world, she turned to Henry, who had come to stand beside her, and said, "Whitelands, indeed."

"Yes. Although I believe the village got its name from the chalk of the hills, and not from snow. It's a pleasant spot. I'm sorry you have received such a bad impression of it."

Paula would have welcomed the chance of talking to Henry on his own because it seemed to her that he could be more easily worked on than his wife, but before she could speak, Louise returned from the cloakroom and Kitty appeared on the stairs.

"Bill's gone to bed," she said. "I've called the doctor's surgery and one of them will look in as soon as possible."

"Is James with him?" asked Paula.

"No. He's in the sitting-room."

Paula found him in one of the big armchairs by the log fire, absent-mindedly stroking the cat, who was lying purring on his lap. He looked up when she came in and made a grimace. "I'm sorry, love."

Paula came over to sit on the arm of the chair.

"Shall I shift the animal?" he asked.

"No. Kitty will be here any moment. The Gravertons are just leaving."

"Lucky them."

"Yes indeed. But it's all right, James. I'm quite reconciled to staying here tonight if they seem to want us to and if you think we should."

"You really mean that?"

"Of course."

"Thank heaven." James moved the cat aside and hugged Paula. "Bill has been begging me not to go. He's perfectly disgusting, but I can't help wondering whether there isn't some justification for his fears."

"That Kitty is trying to get rid of him? Isn't that what we were talking about on the way here?"

James looked even more relieved. "So you don't think he is just being paranoid?"

"I think she's got a very good motive for murder."

"Bless you, darling. I was afraid that you'd—"

Paula put a hand over his mouth. "She's coming. Talk later."

Kitty came into the room and said abruptly, "Do you two want to leave as well? I can't say I'd blame you."

"Paula and I have agreed," replied James, "that if you want us to go we will, and if you want us to stay, we will. It's up to you."

Kitty looked puzzled. "Of course I want you to stay. Anything that comes between husband and wife is a bonus in this house. What's the use of pretending otherwise? But I think you're quite crazy, both of you."

She moved over to the coffee-table, picked up a yellow pottery box that lay there, and offered a cigarette to Paula before helping herself. Her beautiful hands, which had been comparatively

still while she was talking to Paula upstairs, were now once again
in constant motion.

"Oh. I'm sorry, James." Kitty opened the cigarette box again.
"No thanks," said James. And then he added rather plaintively, "I suppose we couldn't have some tea?"

"Of course." Kitty jumped up from the chair on which she
had only just sat down. "China? Indian? Earl Grey?"

"Indian, please. Sure it's not a nuisance?"

Kitty seemed not to have heard him. She gave them one of
her vague smiles, crushed out the cigarette unsmoked, and left
the room.

"I've always believed," remarked James, "that when people
are anxious and apprehensive, they like to be asked to make tea.
It gives them something to occupy themselves."

"I doubt if Kitty is ever short of that. This house doesn't look
after itself, and it looks perfect. I feel I ought to help with clearing up the dining-room."

"Don't you dare. You'll get into a cosy little men-hating session with her and be absolutely intolerable, and I can't stand it at
the moment."

Paula resisted this invitation to start an argument. It was
ground that they had covered many times before, and the only
consensus they ever reached was an agreement to differ.

"I haven't the slightest desire to help her load the dishwasher," she said placidly. "I'd rather play with the cat."

But the black-and-white cat, after sniffing briefly at her ankles,
returned to James.

"You know I always wanted to be a vet," he said. "It was
Grandmama who shoved me into English literature. She thought
I ought to carry on the family tradition."

"Lambing in the snow? Horses that kick and bite? I don't see
you, James."

"And I don't see you standing at the kitchen cooker making
marmalade, but you assure me you were doing just that yesterday."

At that moment Kitty returned with the tea-tray. It's just as well, thought Paula, for in spite of her resolutions, she had been about to make a sharp retort.

"Aren't you going to join us?" she said to Kitty.

Kitty shook her head. "I'd better go up. Bill's being ominously quiet."

As she left the room again, Paula noticed that the fingers of her right hand, which hung by her side, were twisting and clutching more strenuously than ever.

"James," she said softly as he drank his tea, "what do you think we ought to do? Kitty looks on the point of collapse."

"I know. If Bill is really ill, he ought to go to hospital."

"Could we suggest to the doctor," began Paula.

"I think we ought to," said James. "Except that he—or *she*," he added hastily, "must surely know what the situation is here."

Paula got up and moved to the door and opened it and stood there listening. James joined her. There was no sound in the house. They looked at each other in helpless anxiety, all differences temporarily forgotten.

"I find this scary," whispered Paula.

"Me too. I'm going up."

"Thanks, darling." She pressed his hand.

James was about half-way up the stairs when they heard the shouting. It sounded at first like the roar of an animal, and then the words became clear.

"Leave me alone! You murderess!"

Paula caught up with James on the landing, and they pushed at the door of the main bedroom together.

They were just in time to see Bill snatch at the glass of water that Kitty was holding out to him, and fling it at her.

She side-stepped; most of the water went on the carpet, and the glass lay there unbroken. It was as if a petulant child or a senile adult was refusing to feed or drink, and it was, as James had said, repulsive to witness.

Paula and James stood in the doorway. Kitty turned, saw

them, and walked out of the room without giving them another glance and without saying a word. Her hands were working convulsively at her sides. Bill leaned back against the pillows and shut his eyes, apparently exhausted. He was wearing a dark blue dressing-gown and he looked very pale. Perhaps he really was ill; perhaps he really did have cause to be afraid. For the first time since she had entered the house, Paula began to feel a little stirring of pity for him.

James obviously felt the same, for he moved across to the bed and sat down on it and said, "Can I get you anything, Bill?"

There was no response. James leaned down, picked up the glass, sniffed at it, looked back at Paula and shook his head. She signed to him that she was going to follow Kitty, and he nodded. Two suspects, two guards, thought Paula as she walked downstairs; it's all rather ridiculous, but at least James and I are working together.

Kitty was in the dining-room clearing up the lunch table. Paula joined her, not saying anything, and helped to carry the used dishes into the kitchen. During the meal, she herself had been feeling too ill and preoccupied to be observant, but she noticed now that there were indeed several wooden bowls on the table containing the remains of the winter salad—chicory, nuts, grated carrot, apple, and oranges. She had eaten from the bowl that had stood between her place and Henry Graverton's. It was nearly empty, but she could see traces of onion in it.

To the right of Bill's place stood a similar bowl. It looked as if it had hardly been touched. Paula took up one of the salad-servers and stirred the contents. Was there onion? It was difficult to tell. Spurred on by curiosity, she took a clean fork and ate a mouthful from the bowl. No onion. Just the very faintest hint of garlic. This seemed to dispose of one theory: that Bill had eaten from a salad bowl containing onion, or that Kitty had deliberately put some into his bowl, knowing that it would make him ill.

The goulash must surely be innocent. They had all eaten it. Bill had served himself, and the rest of them, from the same dish. What about the potatoes? Henry, Louise, and James appeared to have eaten their baked potatoes, skin and all. Paula had left half of hers, and so had her host and hostess. But there again, Bill's must have been harmless. They had all helped themselves from the dish, and there was no way that Kitty could have known which one Bill would take.

The bread rolls? Similar reasoning applied.

That left only the wine. They had been drinking a rosé, and Bill himself had opened the bottle, as he had done in the case of the drinks they had had before lunch. From her own observation, Paula could see no way in which Kitty could have administered any poisonous substance to Bill during the time that the guests had been in the house. Perhaps he had earlier in the day taken something slow to act; or perhaps he had deliberately eaten something—some of the salad containing onion, for instance—that he knew would make him ill.

Or perhaps the whole thing was just an act. Paula felt that she had done her best and that it was up to the doctor to find out what had really happened. Kitty, who was loading the dishwasher in the kitchen, would be returning to the dining-room any moment now, and Paula did not want to be caught snooping.

She moved over to the sideboard, where there stood a selection of fruit and a cheesecake with a pile of plates alongside. Paula had not eaten much lunch, and it looked very tempting. She remarked on this as Kitty came into the room.

"Help yourself," said Kitty. "It's a pity to waste it."

"Thanks."

"I'll have some too."

They sat down at the window end of the table and ate in silence for a while.

Then Kitty said, "Satisfied with your investigations?"

Paula was rather taken aback, but hoped that she did not show it as she replied, "The doctor is going to want to know what Bill has eaten, and if he continues with his accusations—"

"Yes, I know. I'm sorry, Paula. I'm grateful really. Have some more cheesecake."

"Thanks. It's the best I've ever eaten. If you took a job as a cook, you'd have your salary and you'd be independent."

"I've thought of it, but it wouldn't pay for Marie, any more than the secretarial jobs do. Anyway, it's too late now. I chose the contract with Bill."

Paula could not help wondering how much Bill was paying to meet his side of the bargain. Perhaps James would know. It was hateful to find oneself trying to translate Bill's and Kitty's very different human problems into terms of money, but that was the way of the world. Against her will, Paula found herself suddenly seeing the whole situation from Bill's point of view. Presumably he had believed himself to be paying a great deal of money for an elegant home and hostess and for a constant flattering reflection to maintain his own self-image. Kitty had not accused him of failing to keep his side of the bargain.

But had Kitty been keeping to hers? Could any woman keep to such an agreement?

Paula thought about this as they once again ate in silence, and gave herself the answer: Yes. Countless women in past centuries, and plenty of women even today, had no choice but to make bargains of this nature for the sake of their own survival, and the name of the contract was marriage.

They had no choice. Kitty had had a choice, and she had chosen with her eyes open. Paula knew that never, in no imaginable circumstances, could she herself make such a choice. Not even if it involved the well-being of the creature she loved best in the world. Freedom came first: she could not sell herself into slavery. Perhaps this was selfish, perhaps this was a grave fault in her, but she could never do it, and therefore, in her heart, she could not completely understand and sympathise with Kitty.

But if it were a sick child?

No. She could not do it. She would have to find some other way.

The doorbell rang, but Kitty did not stir.

"Shall I go?" said Paula.

Kitty nodded. "It'll be the doctor. I'll come in a moment."

Paula got up. Did Kitty want to stay behind in order to conceal something or perhaps throw something away? It was impossible not to wonder. Her feelings were all on Kitty's side; but her mind insisted that Kitty had the strongest motive for getting rid of Bill and that she might well be playing a very deep game.

The house was very silent. Apparently James had succeeded in keeping Bill calm. When Paula opened the front door the first thing she saw was that the outside world was whiter than ever. James's car, standing outside the garden gate, was now a smooth mound of snow, and there were no signs of activity in the village street. On the garden path there were deep footprints, not very big footprints and not very far apart.

A woman's voice, light and young-sounding, said, "May I come in, please?"

The girl was standing at the edge of the step, kicking her boots against it to dislodge the snow. She was wearing a scarlet coat with a hood, and underneath the hood was what looked to Paula a very young face with bright brown eyes, dark hair, and a wide, smiling mouth.

She was about Paula's height, not very tall, and she carried a black bag.

"Marilyn Shore, Dr. Mayhew's partner," she said as she stepped into the hall. "You're Mrs. Burden?"

"No. I'm a guest." Paula gave her name. "Mrs. Burden asked my friend and me to stay when Professor Burden was taken ill. She'll be here in a moment. Did you have trouble getting here?"

"I've known worse, but it's probably going to get worse. The road is blocked by a big drift at the far end, and they won't be getting round to clear it today. Boyds Lane isn't too bad. They usually manage to keep that open."

"Where is your surgery?" asked Paula.

"Lewes. We cover quite a big area. I've visited patients in

Whitelands before, but never Professor Burden. I'd better get to him now if Mrs. Burden isn't coming. Where is he?"

"Upstairs," replied Paula, wishing that Kitty would hurry up, but at the same time thinking that it would be interesting to observe Bill's first encounter with Dr. Marilyn Shore.

"What's the matter with him?" asked Dr. Shore as they walked upstairs.

"I don't know. Something he's eaten maybe."

They reached the bedroom door. There was still no sign of Kitty, but James came out onto the landing, introduced himself to the doctor, held open the door of Bill's bedroom for her, and then turned to Paula and pulled a face expressive of delight and alarm.

"I'd better go and give him moral support," he murmured. "Tell you about it later."

Paula had no choice but to retreat.

At least she could tell Kitty that the doctor looked likely to bring an independent and unbiassed judgment to Bill's case. But Kitty was nowhere to be found, neither in the kitchen nor in any of the ground-floor rooms. She could surely not have gone upstairs without being seen, but nevertheless Paula ran up to the top of the house and glanced into Kitty's office and into the bedroom next door.

She then proceeded to search the house and pushed hard at the back door, which would not shift because of the weight of snow piled up against it. Becoming more and more convinced, however, that Kitty had left the house, she returned to the front hall and opened the front door.

The short January day was coming to an end, and the sky was grey and heavy. The falling snowflakes were now small and dry, and on the garden path the doctor's footprints were already becoming blurred.

There seemed to be rather more of them than before.

Shivering slightly with the cold, Paula bent down to look more closely at the part of the doorstep that was beyond the cover of the porch. The snow here was disturbed, but that could have been done by the doctor kicking at the step. On the path between the rose-bushes there was clearer evidence that other feet had walked that way, larger feet than the doctor's but clearly wearing a woman's shoes or boots.

So Kitty had run away. She must have been preparing to do so and had taken her chance during the short time that Paula had been showing Dr. Shore where to find Bill.

Of course, it might be only temporary. She might be going to one of the shops or to the post office before closing time, but Paula didn't think this likely. Kitty was far too efficient a house-keeper to find herself suddenly without some essential item. Per-haps she had just felt the need to get out of the house for a while, whatever the weather. She had been under very great strain: it would not be surprising if she had come to the end of her self-control.

But if that were the case, wouldn't it have been more friendly to have told Paula openly, to have given Paula the chance to try to help her, instead of sneaking off like this.

Perhaps she had left a note.

Paula searched all possible places, but could find none. She felt very tempted, while looking on the table in the sitting-room where the telephone stood, to call the Gravertons and ask if Kitty had taken refuge with them, but after a moment's reflec-tion she decided to hold this in reserve. Kitty might yet return, and meanwhile, there must surely be some news of Bill.

4

"I can't find anything wrong with him," said Dr. Shore, "except an anxiety state. I've sedated him, and he should sleep for a few hours." She glanced at her watch. "I ought to talk to Mrs. Burden. You've no idea when she will be back?"

"None at all," replied Paula. "In fact, I think it's quite likely that she won't be back today."

"So you two have been left holding the baby?"

"Could you spare ten minutes," asked James, "while we explain?"

"I've several more calls to make, but they are none of them very urgent and the weather is an excuse for delay. All right. Thank you, yes, I'd love some coffee."

Paula left James to tell the tale, which he did with admirable speed and clarity.

"So you think Mrs. Burden has chosen this moment to leave her husband," commented Dr. Shore when he had finished.

"No, I don't think so," broke in Paula, and proceeded to explain about the daughter.

"You never told me this," said James reproachfully.

"I've hardly had a chance. I was going to tell you."

"This probably explains her disappearance," said Dr. Shore, putting down her coffee-cup and getting up from her armchair. "My guess is that she has gone to see her daughter. That's the reason why she has put herself into an intolerable situation. Seeing the girl may give her fresh courage and determination to carry on. Do you know where she is?"

Paula, feeling somewhat chagrined that she had not thought of this solution herself, replied that she did not but that surely there must be some record somewhere in the house.

"There's a hospital for severely disabled children, including the mentally handicapped, at Larkfield," said Dr. Shore.

"She wouldn't be there," said Paula. "That's the whole point —not to have her in hospital."

"I was only going to suggest," said Dr. Shore mildly, "that the people there might be able to help us. Caring for such a child, even for a large fee, isn't everybody's idea of the good life. I'll call the hospital for you if you like."

Paula, even more irritated with herself than before, was almost effusive in her thanks. James picked up the tray with the coffee-cups and went out into the kitchen, where Paula followed him.

"Are you all right?" he asked rather anxiously.

"More or less," she replied. "In fact, I'm getting rather fascinated in a morbid sort of way. What is going to happen? How any woman could do what Kitty has done—" Paula paused and shook her head. "It stirs up all one's own hang-ups," she concluded.

"I know," said James sympathetically. "I've felt just the same about Bill—wondering if I wasn't a bit like that myself and feeling quite murderous towards him because of it. By the way, love, don't be misled by Dr. Shore's sparkling eyes and merry smile. She's a little toughie. You should have seen her dealing with the patient."

"I wish I had. I think she's finished. We'd better go back."

Dr. Shore handed Paula a piece of paper on which she had written a couple of telephone numbers. "These are the matron's suggestions. The first one is a Mrs. Matthews. That is a private house. The other is a very expensive little clinic—Woodside. You might like to try them both. I don't think Professor Burden is going to cause you any trouble, especially if his wife doesn't return, but here is my phone number. I could try to get you an agency nurse, but it's not going to be easy at such short notice and with the weather like this."

"I think we can manage," said James.

"I'll leave some sleeping pills with you, in case they are needed. He can take two of them." Dr. Marilyn Shore put on her gloves and pulled up the hood of her coat. "Call me if you need to. I'll be back home by seven-thirty. With luck," she added after looking out of the front door. "Thank goodness my other calls are local ones in Lewes. What sort of car does Mrs. Burden drive?"

James and Paula looked at each other.

"You don't know," said the doctor. "Well, for all your sakes I hope it's a Land-Rover or something similar. There's nothing else going to get through to Whitelands tonight. Goodbye."

She plunged off down the garden path, and they saw her by the light of the lamp at the entrance to the churchyard, brushing the fresh snow off her car.

"Ought we to help?" murmured Paula.

"No," said James firmly, shutting the front door of The Twitten. "It's her job. Would you like to call those phone numbers while I go up and have a look at Bill? I'm going to see if he's got a spare toothbrush. You can go and raid Kitty's cupboards later. I don't see why we shouldn't make ourselves comfortable."

"Neither do I," said Paula.

She returned to the sitting-room and sat down by the telephone table. The first of the numbers was engaged. She tried the second and was told by a very cold and distant female voice that there was nobody answering to her description resident on the premises, that the telephone number was ex-directory, and that no unauthorised person ought to possess it. Paula explained about Dr. Shore's enquiries, but the voice was very little mollified and told Paula that on no account was the number to be given to any other person.

"I haven't the slightest intention of handing it on to anybody," retorted Paula. "The whole business is nothing whatever to do with me, and I've only got caught up in it through trying to help someone."

"Sounds like some sort of luxurious private prison," she muttered to herself as she waited a minute before trying the first number again. The line was no longer busy, but it seemed a long time before anybody spoke, and the voice, when it came, was disconcerting.

"Who is that? What is that?"

It was a nervous little squeaky voice, and it was impossible to tell whether the speaker was young or old, male or female.

"Please may I speak to Mrs. Matthews," said Paula slowly and clearly.

There was no response. She thought for a while that the line had gone dead, and was on the point of giving up when at last a pleasant and businesslike woman came on the line.

"Victoria Matthews here. I am sorry about the delay. My father ought not to have answered the phone. He is not well. Who is it speaking, please?"

Paula gave her name. "I'm staying with Professor and Mrs. Burden at Whitelands. Professor Burden is ill, and the doctor attending him suggested that we might reach Mrs. Burden at your number."

"Mrs. Burden is here," admitted Victoria Matthews, "but she is hardly in a fit state to come home and is certainly not fit to look after her husband. I really do not know what to suggest."

"Is it possible for me to speak to her?"

There was a pause, during which it seemed to Paula that there was a male voice somewhere in the background.

"Excuse me a moment," said Mrs. Matthews. "Don't ring off."

The man's voice became more audible, but Paula could not distinguish any words. James came into the room, and she signed to him to remain silent.

"Dr. Glenning." Mrs. Matthews sounded relieved. "We have a solution to our difficulty. The friend of Mrs. Burden who drove her here in his Land-Rover, will come back right away and explain to you what has been happening and give you any help he can. It will take him about forty minutes. His name is Philip Aston. He is a lawyer, working in London, but he spends a lot of time with his father, who lives alone on one of the big estates in Whitelands."

Paula thanked her, put down the telephone, and repeated the information to James. "Enter a major suspect," she added. "Kitty Burden's friend. She told me she met him when she visited Marie. She didn't say he was partially resident here. In fact, there seems to be quite a lot that she didn't say. Do you think Bill had Philip Aston in mind when he made those remarks at lunch?"

"Probably. Surely he must know about it. Maybe he even fancies this guy for himself."

"Did Bill mention him when he was talking to you, James?"

"I don't think so. He didn't talk about anybody but Kitty and how she was planning to murder him. It got somewhat tedious, to say the least. I've been trying to think, by the way, whether Bill has any relatives or anybody who would come and cope with him if Kitty really is opting out. There's no children, but I believe there is a younger brother somewhere."

Paula made no reply. She gave a big yawn and leaned back in her chair and shut her eyes. The room was warm, and for the first time in many hours there was a feeling of a relaxation of tension. James regarded her with sympathy for a moment or two, and then picked up the copy of the day's *Times* that lay on the coffee-table and turned to the crossword puzzle.

For a quarter of an hour there was silence in the house, apart from the tick of the grandfather clock and the occasional crackling of burning wood in the open grate. Then the front doorbell shrilled. Paula woke with a start and looked around her in bewilderment. The deep gold curtains, the high bookshelves, the sparking fire, and the black-and-white cat settled on James's knee, all looked completely unfamiliar, and it was several seconds before she remembered where she was.

"What's the time?" she asked.

"Just gone six." James put the cat aside and stood up. "That can't be Philip Aston yet."

"Philip Aston?" repeated Paula. She had been dreaming very vividly during her short sleep and was still not fully adjusted to the total immersion into other people's lives of the previous hours. By the time James returned, however, she was once again fully alert and able to greet the man he brought with him, a tallish grey-haired man, rather ascetic-looking, wearing a dark suit and overcoat and a clerical collar.

"Mr. Robert Fulham, vicar of this parish," said James, helping the newcomer to shed his coat. "I've told him briefly what has been happening here, Paula, and I think we could all do with a drink."

"Professor Burden asked me to call round about six o'clock," said Mr. Fulham, accepting a whisky and moving near to the fire. "I believe there was something he wanted to tell me. He sounded very agitated."

"He got more and more so," said Paula. "Would it have been something to do with Mrs. Burden?"

"I'm afraid so." The newcomer sat down, put the glass on the hearthstone, and stretched his hands out gratefully to the glowing wood. "You must have seen for yourselves how it is between them."

Behind his back, Paula and James looked at each other, silently consulting: How much should we tell him?

We are like Henry and Louise Graverton, thought Paula, when they were deciding whether or not to tell me about Bill making scenes and I felt envious of their togetherness. This was a comforting thought. She had been so afraid that the Whitelands affair would cause a rift between James and herself, but it seemed to be doing the opposite: they were coming closer together, and they were reading each other's thoughts: Go carefully; don't say anything about Philip Aston, wait to hear what he has to say, and try to get rid of him before Philip arrives.

"It was a most uncomfortable lunch." Paula joined Mr. Fulham by the fire. "Bill and Kitty were working out their private differences in front of their guests, and I think we all rather resented it."

"I don't blame you," said the vicar. "And it isn't for the first time. Only last week . . ."

And he proceeded to tell the story that Henry Graverton had told, of the committee meeting at The Twitten and the "rat-poison cakes." James had not heard it at all; Paula was interested in the different manner of the telling. Henry and Louise had emphasised the overall unpleasantness of the scene, but the Reverend Robert Fulham seemed to be more interested in the state of mind of the protagonists.

"Of course, I knew it was nonsense," he concluded, "and that there was nothing wrong with Kitty's delicious cakes, but somehow I couldn't bring myself to eat one. It was my sister who did that. She is very worried about Bill. She feels that he ought to be receiving psychiatric help, and I promised her to try to suggest it to him this evening, but you say he is in bed?"

"Fast asleep under heavy sedation," said James. "I'm afraid you're having a wasted visit. Though I take it that you haven't had far to come?"

"Through the churchyard. The vicarage is the other side of it."

"But it must be deep in snow," said Paula, glancing at the vicar's boots, which looked surprisingly dry.

"Glenys and I cleared the path," he said with a smile. "We aren't all that ancient, and we are used to rural life. After ten years in the wilds of Yorkshire a couple of Sussex villages to look after seems like a rest-cure. You might call it a sort of half-way house to retirement."

"Bill Burden came here as a step to retirement too," commented James. "Do you think it was a wise step? Would you say that he had adapted himself to village life? I've known him for years and always thought he was very much a big-city man."

"It was a very unwise step indeed," said Mr. Fulham in a most decided manner. "Even if he had been a country-lover himself, it would still have been most unwise to bring a pretty wife much younger than himself to Whitelands and expect her to be content. If you are moving from town to country, or indeed to anyplace where you know nobody, the first essential is that you should be happy in your home life. A happy couple will soon adapt itself to the community. An unhappy couple can only grow more unhappy and spread its discontent. I'm sorry." Mr. Fulham picked up his glass. "I seem to be preaching a sermon. My only excuse is that I truly care for this little community, and I am afraid that Professor and Mrs. Burden—"

He paused again. James finished the sentence. "Bill and Kitty are not exactly adding to the peace and charm of village life?"

The vicar nodded. "You'll think me very uncharitable, but I can't help wishing they would move elsewhere. Brighton, for instance. Kitty Burden would have much more to interest her, and it's too big a place to be upset by them."

Paula could not help smiling. She found the Reverend Robert Fulham's direct and faintly sardonic manner very refreshing after the falseness and pretentiousness that Bill Burden shed around him.

"How about the other people who live here," she continued. "Would they be pleased if Bill and Kitty moved out of Whitelands?"

"The tradesmen wouldn't. They'd lose some good customers. The good-works gang—my sister's expression, not mine—might be rather torn. They are always glad of support, financial or otherwise, and at first they were delighted to have Professor Burden here. But I suspect that they are beginning to find the price too high, and they are dreading a repetition of last week's committee meeting."

"I don't blame them," said Paula. "How did the people at the

big house react? I forget the name, but the house is called
Boyds, isn't it?"

"Yes. Nobody knows why. Presumably there was at some
time a landowner of that name, but we can find no record of it.
My sister and I are keen on local history. I'd much rather play
about trying to reconstruct the past than try to hold back the
inevitable future."

"Such as better roads?" Paula could not resist saying this, although she feared she was being diverted from her purpose.

"We badly need better roads," said the vicar, accepting more
whisky and speaking with greater seriousness. "The children
walk to school along a lane where there is no footpath. And
every winter we have problems with the snow, as you can see for
yourselves. It causes great hardship to the old people."

"Does Bill Burden know that you don't agree with him on
this matter?" asked James, glancing at Paula as he spoke.

"I don't make any secret of my opinions," retorted the vicar,
"and I don't think Professor Burden bears me any ill will because of them."

"Then who is on the other side?" interposed Paula quickly.
"Who are the genuine preservationists?"

"The Gravertons would like to keep things as they are, and so
would Roger Aston at Boyds. And presumably his son, Philip.
And the Burdens. And the pottery people, Mrs. Reid and her
brood, pretend to agree with them. It's my sister and I who are
the open dissidents."

"Roger Aston," said Paula thoughtfully. "Yes, that's the
name. What sort of man is he?"

"Very conservative, even by Whitelands standards. Very eccentric. Goes about looking like an old tramp, which doesn't
please his son, Philip, who is inclined to be the well-dressed City
man. Philip's a good fellow though. There aren't many successful professional men who would take so much time and trouble
over a rather dotty old father. He's down here nearly every
weekend and sometimes during the week as well."

"Has he always been so attentive?" asked Paula.

"Ever since I've been here. And that's nearly seven years."

So it isn't just since Kitty Burden came to live in Whitelands, thought Paula; I wonder if she knew him in London? Surely not, or why on earth didn't she marry Philip instead of Bill?

The Reverend Robert Fulham was handing James his glass and declining another refill. "I must go. You folks will be glad of a little peace. I'll just go up and take a look at the professor. I won't disturb him if he's asleep. No, there's no need to come too, thanks. I know his room."

After he had gone, James and Paula consulted their watches.

"If Philip arrives—"

"I'll smuggle him into the dining-room. We don't want them to meet."

"What do you make of the vicar?"

"He doesn't like Bill. I doubt if anybody does. And there seem to be feuds in the village."

"Passions run deep. But do they go as far as poison?"

"As far as we know," commented Paula, "nobody has been poisoned. The vicar is being a long time. I hope he hasn't woken Bill."

"Perhaps he's smothering him with a pillow. I don't think we ought to have let him go up."

"We couldn't have stopped him."

By unspoken consent they moved out into the hall and looked up the stairs.

"He's probably praying over him," whispered Paula.

"Bill could do with it. I'm going to look."

But James had only taken a couple of steps before Mr. Fulham appeared, apologising for having been so long and suddenly in a great hurry to leave the house.

"You know where to find us if we can be of any help," he said. "It's stopped snowing at last. I think we are going to have a clear night. Goodbye."

They watched him plod down the path and continue round

the garden wall until he reached the entrance to the churchyard. There he paused for a moment under the lamp and seemed to be examining something at his feet before he finally set off through the lych-gate and up the steep path between the gravestones.

"We've been in this house for six hours," said James, going to the cloakroom, "and it feels like a week. I'm going out for a breath of fresh air. Coming?"

Paula was already pulling on a pair of Kitty's boots. "Ought we to have a look at Bill?"

"Damn Bill. Do stop fussing, Paula. We can leave the door unlocked. There won't be any burglars on a night like this, and in any case, we're not going out of sight of the house."

They came out of the front gate and surveyed the white mound that was James's car.

"Shall we dig it out now?" suggested Paula. "Then it will be ready for us in the morning."

"There's no hurry," he replied. "I doubt if we'll get away very early. This must be Boyds Lane."

He walked a few yards to the left of The Twitten. Their eyes were becoming adjusted to the darkness, and the snow produced its own sort of strange light. On either side of an opening in a low stone wall were gateposts, and to the left-hand one was attached a five-bar gate, pushed right back and held back by the weight of snow.

From the condition of the track, it looked as if quite a number of vehicles had recently passed that way.

"Very revealing," remarked James, "if one had an expert knowledge of tyres. Can you see the house?"

"Boyds, you mean? I think it's behind that clump of trees."

"Perhaps Philip will stop there first and see his dad. I suppose we'd better go back now."

But Paula seemed inclined to linger. "The vicar is right. It's turning into a lovely starry night. Let's go and look at the churchyard. It's so beautifully eerie. You can carry on with your Sherlock Holmes act there."

They walked back past the Burdens' house. All was exactly as they had left it, and there was no sign of life in the village. At the low wooden entrance of the lych-gate, Paula paused for a moment. "The vicar was looking at something near here."

"Dr. Shore brushed the snow off her car and skidded a bit while getting started," said James, straightening up from his investigations to find that Paula had disappeared. She called to him from among the yew-trees and ancient gravestones under the high wall of the churchyard that was nearest to the Burdens' house. It was indeed an eerie spot.

"My feet are freezing," grumbled James.

"Ssh. Can you hear a car coming?"

"I can see the lights." James was looking over the wall. "It's coming along Boyds Lane. We'd better go."

"No. Let's wait a moment."

The lights approached slowly.

"He'll have to park where the doctor did," murmured James. "There's nowhere else clear enough."

They waited in the shadows, well beyond the range of the lamp by the gate, while the Land-Rover drew up where James had said it would.

"He's not alone," whispered Paula.

Somebody was getting out of the passenger seat.

"It's Kitty."

"Ssh."

She was wearing a long cloak of some dark material, and its hood had slipped back to reveal her face, which was turned towards the churchyard. It looked ghastly in the greenish lamplight. The driver came from the other side of the car and put an arm round her. He spoke in a low voice, but they could hear the words clearly. There was no other sound in the village.

"Are you quite sure you want to go back? Wouldn't you rather stay with my father?"

Kitty's reply was equally clear. "I'll be all right now. I've got to see it through. It won't take long."

"You won't change your mind?"

"Not now. Never again. I have to be free."

"If I could only do it for you— Don't you trust me?"

"Of course I trust you. But this is something I have to do alone."

They moved away towards the gate of The Twitten. Paula and James could still hear their voices but could no longer distinguish any words.

"Are you thinking what I am thinking?" whispered Paula.

"I am indeed. And it rather sounds as if they have forgotten that we are staying for the night."

As they came up to the white mound that was James's car, he stretched out an arm and brushed a swathe of snow from the windscreen.

"We can still escape along Boyds Lane. A cinema and a late dinner in Brighton. Doesn't that appeal?"

"Enormously. But we can't go now. Suppose they really are planning to finish off Bill? And in any case, I want to know what Philip is like. Hurry up. They're shutting the door."

5

Philip Aston looked rather like the young Elvis Presley, but with greying hair and a supercilious expression. Paula could sense James's instant dislike of him and had no doubt that the feeling was returned with interest. They regarded each other as suspiciously as tomcats meeting on neutral territory, while Paula spoke to Kitty.

"How is Bill?" asked Kitty.

She looked scarcely less ghastly in the soft pinkish lights of the sitting-room than she had under the streetlamp. It was as if the mask had broken up completely. Only her voice, brusque and faintly mocking, reminded Paula of the slick hostess and of the unhappy woman who had confided in her.

"I think he's still asleep," replied Paula. "The doctor gave him a heavy sedative. She said there was nothing wrong with him except anxiety."

"Is that all?"

There was no mistaking the note of disappointment.

Philip turned away from James, who had just been explaining, at unnecessary length, that he and Paula had been accompanying the vicar home, and put an arm round Kitty in a proprietary manner.

"Come on. I'll come up with you. You can see for yourself that he's all right, and then you had better go to bed. I'm sure Paula will have found her way about the kitchen and will make you some supper if you want it."

He's as bad as Bill, thought Paula. How can Kitty stand it? She really is a mystery.

Kitty allowed herself to be hustled away, but at the door she turned and gave Paula a look of such hopeless appeal that the latter said, more warmly than she had intended, "I'll come up later. Will you be in your little room?"

Kitty nodded almost imperceptibly. Paula had the strong impression that she was silently crying out for help, and remarked on this to James when the others had gone.

But James was more concerned about Bill. "I want to have a look at him before they do," he muttered, "but I don't want to make it too obvious. Have they gone right up to the top of the house? Can you hear anything?"

They had moved out into the hall, and Paula was standing at the foot of the stairs, clinging to the bannisters and craning her neck to try to see the upper landings. She untwisted herself and shook her head. "I can't see where they've gone."

"Never mind. I'll just have to risk a confrontation."

With considerable anxiety, Paula watched him run upstairs two steps at a time. Philip Aston's arrival, which they had been half-consciously hoping would relieve them of responsibility, had greatly increased the sense of tension in the house. All James's suppressed irritation was ready to break out at the least excuse, and Paula almost wished that they had given way to their momentary impulse to dig out the car and flee. Then she remembered the look on Kitty's face and knew that she could not abandon her.

Somebody was coming down from the top floor. Paula, halfway up the stairs herself, saw with relief that it was Philip. With luck she would be able to keep him and James apart.

"Does Kitty want anything?" she asked.

"Not at the moment. But I would like to talk to you." He glanced around as he came to the landing. "Alone, please."

The tone was peremptory. Paula bit back a sharp retort. "James has gone to sit with Bill," she said as they came into the sitting-room. "He's an old friend of Bill's, you know, and is very much upset about the situation here."

"I'm a friend of both of them, and I'm also very upset," said Philip grimly. "They can't go on like this. It's got to end." He picked up the whisky bottle. "Sorry; I never offered you—"

Paula refused with equal abruptness. "What did you want to tell me?"

"About Kitty. She's on the verge of total breakdown. She *is* in total breakdown. Mrs. Matthews wanted to get her into hospital, and I had great difficulty in persuading her to let me bring her here."

"Wouldn't it perhaps have been better," ventured Paula, since he seemed to be expecting her to comment.

"In some respects, yes. But then the whole story would have to come out. Doing it this way, we may be able to hush it up."

"To hush what up?" cried Paula. "What are we talking about?"

"About Kitty's attempt to kill her daughter, of course. Didn't Mrs. Matthews tell you?"

"No." Paula sat down, suddenly feeling very weak. "I think I'll have that whisky after all."

"I'm sorry," said Philip, offering it with something approaching courtesy. "I thought you knew."

After a moment's pause, during which both of them drank and rearranged their thoughts, Philip continued.

"I came down from London early this afternoon to make sure that my father was warm and comfortable. He forgets to turn up the heating and won't let anybody look after him—but that's my problem. About four o'clock, or a little earlier, I had just decided that I would have to stay overnight, when Kitty turned up, very distraught and saying that she had to go and see Marie immediately. Normally I drive her over at weekends. Kitty doesn't drive. There is some deep-rooted problem there that she does not choose to tell anybody about. Bill was very relieved when I took over this job from him. He didn't want to have to see Marie, but felt that he ought to. He is one of those people who finds mental or physical disability very hard to stomach.

Actually Marie is not particularly repulsive. She is a little round pudding of a body in a wheelchair, with a little round pudding of a head, tiny oriental features, and a black cap of hair. Mrs. Matthews has an old father almost completely senile. He and the child spend the days together. They appear to communicate in some way unknown to the rest of us."

He stopped and took another drink. Paula lit a cigarette and listened avidly, hoping that James would not choose this moment to return.

"Mrs. Matthews looks after them both with the help of one resident nurse and one daily assistant. She herself is a trained nurse. Very competent. The house is isolated. A converted farmhouse, not unlike my father's, but rather smaller, and there is no estate to be kept up, only a garden. I do not know what fee she charges for looking after Marie. I imagine it is very high indeed. Kitty refuses to discuss it. Bill Burden is a rich man, but the double responsibility of Marie and of the house in Whitelands must be very considerable. That's the background.

"I tried to persuade Kitty not to go to see Marie this afternoon. It always distresses her, and today she was already so agitated that it seemed very unwise, but she insisted. Mrs. Matthews was having problems with her father, the resident nurse was in bed with flu, and the daily help, who had driven into Lewes to do the shopping, was delayed because of the weather. We had come at a very awkward time, but Kitty was beyond noticing that. She barely stopped to greet Mrs. Matthews before rushing off to the day-room to see Marie. I tried to smooth things down by offering to clear some of the snow from the drive—it had scarcely been touched. Mrs. Matthews was beginning to look slightly less harassed, when the old man tottered in and embarked on a totally incomprehensible speech. Mrs. Matthews asked me to keep an eye on him while she went to investigate, and a little later she came back with her right hand grasping Kitty firmly by the arm and in her left hand a hypodermic syringe."

Paula gave a little exclamation.

"Yes," said Philip. "That's how I felt. I hadn't the slightest idea that Kitty had it with her. She has completed a couple of years of nurse's training, by the way, in between secretarial jobs. Mrs. Matthews pushed her into a chair, and Kitty broke down completely. She didn't want Marie to suffer; she only wanted Marie to be at peace for ever. The syringe contained diamorphine—a lethal dose. Mrs. Matthews started off by saying that she ought to inform the police; then she calmed down a little and suggested phoning the doctor who attends her own father and Marie. Kitty had by now begun to come out of her fit of madness and to realise what she had done. She was horrified. It seemed to me that the best thing was for me to get her away, and in the end Mrs. Matthews agreed.

"Sometime during the course of the discussion your telephone call came, and the old man picked up the phone. You know the rest, except that on the drive back I talked to Kitty very earnestly indeed, and she agreed that the situation was untenable and that she would have to take drastic action. She suggested herself that the time had come when she would have to tell Bill she was going to leave him and that Marie would have to be removed to a less expensive form of care where she herself would never be left alone with Marie. That's where we now stand, but Bill, it seems, is unfit to be told," concluded Philip on a note of exasperation.

He was staring at the log fire, twisting an empty glass between his fingers. Restless hands, like Kitty's, thought Paula as she digested what had been said. Neither of them realised that a third person had come into the room until they heard him speak.

"And what is it that Bill is unfit to be told?"

He came forward into the room, looking very sleek and composed in the dark green dressing-gown, poured himself some sherry, and took the empty armchair by the fireside.

James, appearing much more agitated than his host, followed him into the room and looked apologetically at Paula and Philip.

"I couldn't stop him. He insisted on coming down."

"It is a curious sensation," remarked Bill suavely, "being talked about as if one were an animal or an inanimate object, in one's own house. But do please go on. I might hear something of interest."

James, standing behind him, made a grimace of despair, and Paula got to her feet. "I ought to go and see if Kitty wants anything. Glad you're feeling better, Bill. Philip will tell you what we were talking bout."

"I'll join you," said James, and they escaped from the room together and shut the door firmly behind them.

"Philip has just told me," began Paula, but James was already on the stairs.

"Later," he called down. "I want to check on something first."

"I'm going up to see Kitty."

He made no reply.

Paula proceeded to the attic floor and knocked on the door of Kitty's little room. There was no reply, and she pushed it open and walked in. The centre light was switched on, but there was no sound of life, and for a moment Paula thought that Kitty was not there.

Then she looked more closely at the divan bed and discovered that the dark mound at the furthest end of it was in fact Kitty, lying curled up under her hooded cloak, her face barely visible. With a renewed sense of shock, Paula came nearer. Kitty ought to be resting in bed. She had gained the impression from Philip, who had come up with her, that Kitty had gone straight to bed.

Paula stretched out a hand and shifted the hood of the cloak, which was almost covering the face. The dark mound did not stir.

Was she breathing?

The answer was yes, but very slowly and unevenly. The pulse was feeble, the skin clammy an cold. Paula cursed her own lack of medical knowledge. Her guess was that Kitty had taken some very strong narcotic, but whether she just needed to sleep it off or whether she had taken too much, Paula could not judge.

The hypodermic, she thought as she ran downstairs. Had Philip said whether they had brought it back with them? Surely Mrs. Matthews had kept it, but in any case, it seemed that Kitty had access to drugs. One the first landing, she ran into James coming out of Bill's room. He started to tell her something, but she interrupted him.

"We must get that doctor back—quick! It looks as if Kitty's overdosed."

"Christ! What next?" exclaimed James and continued to speak, but Paula was not attending.

"Phone in Bill's study," she said breathlessly as she continued on down the stairs. The sitting-room door was still closed, and from behind it came the sound of voices. Next to the cloakroom was Bill's study, a model of a scholar's room for a stage set, elegant and scarcely used. The telephone stood on the leather-topped desk.

Dr. Shore answered at once, listened to Paula's concise explanation of what Kitty had been doing, and asked questions that Paula was unable to answer.

"There was no bottle, no syringe, nothing that I could see to show what she had taken," she was saying, when James, who had been trying to attract her attention, stretched out a hand for the phone.

"Ask her about the sleeping-pills she left for Bill," he said. "They've disappeared."

"Ask her yourself," said Paula, handing over the phone.

"You left me an envelope," said James, "with a few tablets to give to Professor Burden if he became agitated again, and I put it on the shelf below the mirror in his bathroom. He's not taken them himself; he knows nothing about them. I can't find them anywhere. Could Mrs. Burden—"

"I'll try to get an ambulance," interrupted Dr. Shore. "And I'll be over as soon as I possibly can. Is Boyds Lane passable?"

"Yes. It's stopped snowing."

James proceeded to thank her, but she had already rung off.

"She told me to keep her warm," said Paula. "I'll fill some hot-water bottles. Are you going to tell the others?"

"We ought to have told them before," said James. "Philip might know what Kitty has taken."

"Ask him then," snapped Paula. "And call the doctor back. I'm going up to Kitty."

She knew there was nothing she could do, but she could not endure to be doing nothing. In the bathroom opposite Kitty's room she found hot-water bottles, heated water in the kettle that Kitty had used to make their tea so many hours ago, and tucked the hot bottles under the cloak at Kitty's feet.

The room was warm, but Paula was shivering. Kitty had not stirred. The pulse and the breathing seemed to Paula feebler than ever. You have to walk them up and down, to keep them moving, she said to herself. But how do you do that when they are deeply unconscious?

She knelt by the divan; she rubbed the clammy hands. She was crying aloud, although she did not know it.

"Kitty— Oh, Kitty, come back! Please come back! We'll find another way out."

She looked at her watch. Only ten minutes since she had told the doctor. How long would the ambulance take? Ten minutes? Twenty?

Kitty was dying, and there was nothing that Paula could do. And all these hours they had been worrying about the risk to Bill and never once thought that there could be danger for Kitty.

Why had it never occurred to her or to James that Kitty, pushed to the limit, might try to kill herself?

Paula gave herself the answer even as she asked the question: Kitty would never take this way out so long as her daughter lived. Driven to extremes, driven temporarily out of her mind, Kitty had tried to kill Marie, and had she succeeded, she might well have turned upon herself. But she would not kill herself so long as Marie needed her. That fact was as sure as that night follows day.

Paula stood up and began to search around the room with renewed energy. Whatever drugs Kitty had taken, she had not taken them with the intention of dying. She might have made a mistake, but given her nursing experience, that seemed unlikely; or she might have swallowed a tranquilliser to ease herself and, confused from its effects, might have swallowed more.

Or somebody else might have been involved.

Philip had been the last to see her. Why had he left her alone if she had been at such risk? But on the other hand, why should Philip wish Kitty dead?

Perhaps he was tiring of her troubles; perhaps he wanted to be rid of her. Very possible, but surely not a motive for murder. Surely Philip could find a less drastic way of shedding his responsibility.

On the other hand, if he wanted Kitty out of the way, how easy it would be just to let her do the deed herself.

Paula stared at the desk. On it stood Kitty's typewriter, a wire tray in which lay some papers, a full ashtray, the telephone extension, a memo pad, the electric kettle that Paula had just used, an empty milk carton, and the two mugs from which they had earlier drunk their tea.

Kitty had drunk from the dark blue mug, Paula from the light. There was about an inch of liquid left in the bottom of each. They had been interrupted by the Gravertons while drinking their refills and had not finished them; nor had they washed up the mugs.

Cold tea with milk in it: a most unappetising drink, but it would serve to swallow tablets. Or Kitty might have taken them in the bathroom, using the mug that held a couple of toothbrushes.

Paula inspected the bathroom. There was an avocado suite, lemon yellow walls and bathmat, low stool, long mirror, shelf, and wall cabinet. All was neat and adequate, but not luxurious.

This conformed with what Paula believed she now knew of Kitty's character: she put on a show purely for Bill's sake, as part of her 'job,' but her own tastes were very modest.

The mug holding the two toothbrushes still stood on the shelf, and there was no other mug or glass in sight. Paula looked at the wall cabinet, hesitated for a moment, and then pulled at the handle. It opened at once. There were three shelves. At the bottom were soap, bath salts, and similar items. The middle shelf held a variety of widely used remedies for minor ailments, and at the top were bandages and dressings. Paula could see nothing that one would not expect to find in any ordinary household. Presumably Kitty kept supplies of more-potent drugs in a less accessible place.

As Paula came out of the bathroom onto the landing outside Kitty's room, she heard the front doorbell ring, and she gave a little sigh of relief. The doctor. Or the ambulance. At least Kitty would now be in expert hands. Suddenly it occurred to her that Kitty would need night-clothes and toilet items if she were to stay in hospital, and she began to search for them in the closet on the landing where Kitty kept her clothes.

She had got no further than taking a night-gown out of a drawer when she heard a man's voice behind her, quietly speaking her name. She turned round and saw a tall man, slightly stooping, with greying hair and large spectacles. She knew that she knew him, but so keenly had her hope and thoughts been concentrated on help for Kitty that it took her a few seconds to recognise Henry Graverton.

"Hasn't the doctor come?" she asked.

"Not yet. Is there anything I can do?"

"Come and look at her."

It was a relief to Paula to have human company, but in the midst of her intense anxiety she could not help feeling disappointed that James had not come upstairs.

"Do you know anything bout these matters?" she asked as

they stood together looking down at the huddled form under the cloak.

"Not much." He looked very distressed. "I wish we had been more supportive of Kitty, but Louise—"

He broke off. Paula finished the sentence silently: Louise was a little bit jealous of Kitty. So the perfectly harmonious marriage of the Gravertons was perhaps not quite so perfect after all.

"She is a heavy smoker," Henry was saying. "I believe that can increase the effect of a drug."

"But Kitty would know that?"

"Presumably."

"Would anybody else know? Bill, for instance?"

"Paula." Henry was looking around the room, as she herself had done, for some sort of clue as to what had happened. "Are you suggesting—"

"Bill's wide awake now. He could have been pretending to be asleep all the time. He could have come up here when I was talking to Philip." But then she hastily corrected herself. "No, he couldn't have. James would have seen him."

"But why on earth should Bill give Kitty an overdose?"

"If he's genuinely afraid she's trying to poison him . . ."

Paula's voice faded away as Henry did not respond, and she wished she had never made the suggestion. Discretion was rather alien to her nature, but she would not have spoken so freely to a new acquaintance if she had not been so worried and distressed. What did she know about Henry Graverton? Already she was having to revise her first impression of him and his wife. For all she knew, they might be more deeply involved with the Burdens than they had admitted. Why should Louise be jealous if Henry had not given her some cause?

For a moment or two this minor concern drew Paula's mind away from the deep anxiety about Kitty, but when the front doorbell rang again, all other thoughts disappeared in the great flood of relief.

This time it really was the ambulance, and the doctor, too, it seemed, from the sound of voices coming from below. Henry was still looking round the room, actually opening the drawers of Kitty's desk. Paula was at Kitty's side, holding the frighteningly cold hand, willing her to hold on to life.

Dr. Shore came in first, took Paula's place, and looked her up enquiringly.

"We can't find any sign of what she's taken," said Paula. "Could it possibly be—"

"Some natural cause? No, I don't think so. We'll do our best."

Then the men with the stretcher came in, and Paula's relief blended into a surprising sense of loss as they took Kitty away.

6

The evening seemed to go on for ever.

Philip followed the ambulance in his Land-Rover, having promised to telephone from the hospital as soon as there was any news to report. Henry Graverton disappeared without having taken leave of anybody, and the vicar came back, this time accompanied by his sister, Glenys.

Bill welcomed them warmly and also welcomed a plump little middle-aged woman who rang the bell soon afterwards and who turned out to be Mrs. Elizabeth Reid, owner of the Pottery and a member of the Whitelands Preservation Society committee. An ambulance in the snow was apparently not an everyday event in the village community, and Paula had no doubt that the telephone lines were humming.

Bill seemed to be in his element playing the part of the deeply distressed husband.

Or perhaps it was not all pretence. Perhaps Bill really did love Kitty very much. After all, Paula had only Kitty's word for it that his interests lay more in his own sex. James, who had known him for years, had never remarked on it. Why should one not give Bill the benefit of the doubt, as the vicar's sister, Glenys Fulham, seemed to be doing?

She was a neat little lady, wearing a pale blue home-knitted dress and jacket. She accepted a cup of tea from Paula, seated herself in a chair next to Bill, dealt quickly with his apologies for still being in his dressing-gown, and prepared to listen to him. Paula, under pretence of rearranging the tea-tray, kept within earshot. James and the vicar were at the other side of the fireplace talking to Mrs. Reid.

"They think she has taken an overdose," Paula heard Bill say, "but I can't believe it. Surely Kitty wouldn't do that, would she, Glenys?"

He sounded bewildered, even rather pathetic. Could this possibly be acting?

"I don't think she would do it intentionally," Glenys replied, and Paula noticed that she had an exceptionally pleasing voice, soft, calm, and reassuring. "But you know, Bill, it is very easy to make a mistake with tablets, even if one is not feeling very upset about something. Robert and I always count the tablets if one of us has to have a course of antibiotics, and put each day's dose into a separate container. We are dreadfully fussy, but we think it is a sensible precaution."

"It sounds very sensible to me," said Bill. "I'm nervous about pills, Glenys." He lowered his voice so that Paula could only just hear the next words. "Did you know that my mother killed herself that way?"

Paula could not hear Glenys Fulham's reply, and she moved away from the tea-tray then, ashamed of her eavesdropping but at the same time longing to know what they were saying.

James had never mentioned this tragic incident in Bill Burden's life. But then he had probably never heard of it. Men never did know that sort of thing about each other. James was telling Mrs. Reid about Kitty, saying that she had returned from visiting her daughter very tired and distressed and not wanting to talk to anybody. He glanced at Paula as he spoke, as if appealing to her for help.

"Kitty was very upset at lunch-time," said Paula, "and then Professor Burden was taken ill . . ."

"And these two unfortunate souls," said the Reverend Robert Fulham, "have been coping with the household ever since, Mrs. Reid. Not the sort of thing one expects when one comes down from London to lunch with friends in the country."

James and Paula began to speak at the same time, protesting that they only wanted to be of help.

"Ah yes, we all want to be of help," said the vicar. "The desire to help and the desire to know what is going on—can one ever completely separate the two?"

"I won't pretend that I don't want to know what is going on," said Mrs. Reid self-defensively, "but that wasn't the main reason why I came here. I didn't expect to find a house full of people. I heard that Mrs. Burden had been taken to hospital, and I thought that Professor Burden might like to know that his neighbours were thinking of him."

"Very commendable, my dear Elizabeth," said the vicar. "Glenys and I felt just the same. Except that you must allow us an even larger measure of curiosity, since we did in fact know that these good folk here were holding the fort. Although it rather looks," he went on, since his hearers, finding nothing to say, had not taken advantage of his short pause, "as if the only person who is really being of any use to Professor Burden is my sister. As usual."

They all looked across the room to where Glenys was listening to Bill.

That's the one Bill ought to have married, thought Paula suddenly. She's probably rather older than he is, but what does that matter? She would have taken him on as a job, as Kitty did, but she would have done it gladly, determined to make the very best of Bill and finding her own satisfaction in doing so. A good old-fashioned wife, none of this feminist nonsense about her. If only Bill could have met Glenys Fulham before he married Kitty . . .

But Kitty might well be dying at this very moment. And then Bill would be free—rich and free. Glenys? The vicar's sister? Don't be absurd, Paula told herself. She can't possibly have anything to do with Kitty's overdose; she hasn't even been in the house since we've been here, not until she arrived just now.

Her brother had been in the house though and had actually

gone upstairs and lingered there for quite a long time. Again Paula told herself to curb her wild imaginings. Robert Fulham certainly did not fit into the conventional picture of a parish priest, but that was largely because he possessed an uncomfortable sort of honesty and gave the impression of seeing more clearly into people's hearts and minds than was quite acceptable. He had admitted to disliking Bill, but he wanted to be rid of both Bill and his wife, not just of Kitty.

It was all too nonsensical for words, but nevertheless Paula could not get the notion out of her mind.

Had Bill thought of it too? Would he like to have Kitty out of the way so that he could marry Glenys?

Now that was far more likely. In fact, it fitted in perfectly. Look at it from Bill's point of view. The marriage to Kitty has been a disappointment. He has a perfect hostess for public show, but is very much lacking in a sympathetic ear for private consolation. And she is terribly expensive. Perhaps he has financial worries that he is too proud to admit.

They move to Whitelands, and he meets, among other people, his ideal partner, an elderly lady, not glamorous but with great natural dignity. The vicar's sister, a woman of sterling character, universally respected, who also happens to be a sensitive and kind-hearted woman.

If Kitty were out of the way he could marry Glenys. How to get rid of Kitty? Divorce? Kitty might agree to that, provided he continued to pay for Marie, but it wouldn't look good. Two failed marriages within a few years. No. It would make him look foolish and could well lose him Glenys. Nevertheless, he plays with the idea, actively encouraging Kitty's friendship with Philip Aston.

Kitty falls into that trap, but shows no sign of wishing to terminate the marriage. Bill must take more drastic measures. Supposing he can make it appear that Kitty is trying to get rid of him. Lovely youngish wife and rich elderly husband—a classic motive for murder. It casts him in the role of victim, not something that he relishes, but he knows he is only acting and that really it is Kitty who is being victimised.

So on goes the poisoning-accusation campaign, and it is very successful. If he can make everybody believe that Kitty is trying to kill him, then the marriage will most certainly collapse, and nobody can say it is his fault. He probably has no intention of murdering Kitty; he is just waiting to see how things develop before finally deciding what to do.

The doctor's sedation makes him sleepy, but he does not actually sleep; he only pretends to. He knows pretty well what is going on in the house. He knows that Kitty is being driven beyond endurance. And then he sees his chance. A fake suicide. Everything, above all Kitty herself, has played into his hands. Nobody will believe that Kitty has not overdosed. He has opportunity to tamper with her drugs. He knows her life through and through.

All these thoughts were racing through Paula's mind as she appeared to be listening intelligently to what the vicar was saying, still on the subject of the double-edged motives of charitable persons.

Had Bill succeeded? Was Kitty at this very moment breathing her last?

"I wish Philip would phone," she said aloud, interrupting a remark from Mrs. Reid.

"So do I," said Mrs. Reid, not at all sorry to be diverted into speaking the thought that was in all their minds. "It must be terrible for Professor Burden, this waiting."

"It must indeed." Though possibly not quite in the way you mean, added Paula in her own mind.

She glanced across the room. Glenys was talking now, and Bill, looking very pale indeed, was leaning back in his chair and listening to her. I am quite sure that my interpretation is correct, said Paula to herself, and that if Kitty dies, Bill will marry Glenys. And her brother knows this, and that is why he doesn't like Bill, but neither of them has any suspicion of Bill, because they don't like Kitty either.

"I suppose we could call the hospital," James was suggesting.

"Philip said he'd let us know," said the vicar.

There was a silence. Glenys stopped talking, and she and Bill looked across at the other group.

"Would somebody call them, please," said Bill faintly. "This waiting. I don't think I can stand it much longer."

Paula was the first to move. "I'll use the phone in the study," she said as she left the room.

It was now eleven o'clock, one and a half hours since the ambulance had taken Kitty away. She found the number, and after several changes of voice at the other end of the wire, she spoke at last to a nurse who seemed to know what was happening.

"Dr. Brown is with Mrs. Burden now," she said. "Would you hold on a moment."

Paula held on for some time, sitting at Bill's splendid desk in his equally impressive leather-covered desk chair.

If Kitty is dead and they bring in a verdict of suicide, she said to herself, then I am going to have to do something. I don't know what. But I just won't believe it. If Kitty is dead . . .

A voice came on the line at last. It was Philip's.

"Who is that speaking? Oh, Paula. Thank you. I was going to call in a minute. They think she'll pull through."

"Oh, Philip!"

Paula could barely speak.

"I won't tell you the gory details. It's been touch and go, and she's terribly weak. There could be a relapse."

"What was it, Philip?"

"A sort of drugs-and-drinks cocktail, I believe. Deadly mixture, helped on by nicotine—her heavy smoking, you know. Do you want to talk to the nurse?"

"No. There's no need. Philip, I must go and tell Bill. What shall I say?"

"What I've just told you. What else?"

Paula felt sure, from the tone of his voice, that Philip did not in any way share her suspicions about Bill.

"Are you coming back here yourself?" she asked.

"I don't know yet. I'll stay on here for a while and see how Kitty goes on. If she's fit for it, I'd like to see her."

"Oh, yes. If she could see a friendly face—"

"And then I'd better see how my father is. Has he turned up at The Twitten yet?"

"No. Do you expect him to? In this weather? At this hour?"

"You don't know my father. He likes to know what's going on. I'm surprised you've not seen him. Would you do me a kindness, Paula, and look after him if he does turn up. Either you or James. I'm sorry to trouble you with this extra nuisance. You must be longing to get some rest."

"Aren't we all? But the main thing is Kitty. Are they quite sure?"

"Well—medical caution, you know. But there seems a very good hope."

"Thank God. I'll tell Bill. Will you call again?"

"Not unless there's any change. I'll go straight to Boyds, and if my father's not there, I'll come and collect him."

"Thanks, Philip."

Paula put the phone down and sat for a few moments at Bill's desk, trying to calm herself before facing the others.

Kitty would live. That was most important of all. And at least in hospital she was safe. But when she came home? I must do something, thought Paula more and more desperately. I'm sure she's in danger. I must warn her. Unless she knows already?

Her mind began to race again. I'm overtired, she tried to tell herself. I'm not fit to decide anything. I must stop thinking about it tonight.

She had lingered in the study too long. The door opened and James came in.

"Why haven't you—" he began reproachfully and then saw her face. "Paula! What is it, love? Is she dead?"

"No. They think she'll live."

"Thank God."

"James, could you tell the others? I'm not feeling well. Philip will call again if there's any change, but there seems to be every hope. I'm going upstairs to rest for a while. Back bedroom on the first floor. The one we decided to use."

"You go to bed. I'll come up presently."

"And Philip said his father might turn up."

"Why?"

"Curiosity. Hang on to him till Philip comes. And James—"

"Yes, love?"

"Could you watch Bill when you tell him about Kitty? Really watch him. I'll be very interested to know how he reacts."

"I'll do my best. Although I haven't quite your capacity for free interpretation."

"Or imagination," said Paula, trying to smile. "See you later."

She had expected to lie awake and relive the day in a nightmarish tumult of memories and suspicions, but in fact, she fell asleep the moment she lay down. It seemed only minutes later that James spoke to her again, although he assured her that it was nearly seven o'clock in the morning.

"Tea," he added, putting a little white china cup into her hands as if he had performed a conjuring trick.

"How— What—" began Paula, nearly letting it drop.

"Bill insisted on giving us his Teasmade. I'll have to make some more for him, but not just yet."

"Bill." The whole of yesterday, including the final suspicions and her determination to act on them, came flooding back into Paula's mind. She would not tell James about them just yet, but would wait to hear what he had to say.

"Any more news of Kitty?" she asked.

"Only that all is well. I called the hospital just before I woke you up. They'll keep her in a few days."

"Have you been to sleep at all, James?"

"Oh, yes. The party broke up soon after midnight, in spite of Roger's attempts to keep it going."

"Roger?" Paula was momentarily at a loss.

"Philip's father. He turned up some time after you had gone to bed. Extraordinary-looking guy. Looks like a Viking warrior. Apparently has very high blood pressure and is liable to pop off any moment. He doesn't like Bill any more than the vicar does, but the way. He came barging into the room and went straight over to Bill and accused him of driving his wife to suicide. Very embarrassing. Everybody was stunned. Then he added, 'Murder —that's what it is. Nothing short of murder.' "

Paula very nearly said, I'm inclined to agree with him, but restrained herself and asked instead what happened next.

"Glenys calmed him down," replied James. "The indispensable Glenys. She told him that it was much too early to jump to conclusions, that none of us knew yet what had really happened, could well have been an accidental overdose, and so on, and so forth. She and her brother were going home now, and it was time Bill got some rest, and she would come over in the morning to see if he needed her help."

"All this fussing over Bill."

"Yes indeed. I didn't forget your instructions. I kept a watch on him when I brought the news that Kitty would pull through."

"And?"

"I don't know." James was passing a hand over his eyes as if he had a headache. "I'm not much good at these subtleties of expression and reaction. I don't think he looked as I would look if I'd feared you were dying and somebody told me you weren't."

"Ah, but then you've never been very good at hiding your feelings, James. That's why I love you, in spite of everything."

"Is it really? Good Lord, I never knew."

"We'll talk about it some time if you really want to. Although on the whole I think feelings are better left undiscussed."

James began to laugh. "And that's why I love you, since we are on the subject. Most women like to talk about feelings for ever. It's true. You can't deny it. Including the militant feminists. They just have different feelings, that's all."

"I'm afraid it is true. But Kitty isn't like that. Some people would think her hard. But I like her. I want her to get out of her trap and to be herself."

"With Philip?"

Paula looked doubtful, but said, "If that's what she wants. But you haven't told me how Bill did react."

"There's really nothing much to tell," said James. "I came back into the sitting-room, and I said something like, 'Kitty's going to get better,' and as far as I could see, they all looked a bit stupid, as if they couldn't take it in. Then somebody—Mrs. Reid, I think—said, 'Thank God,' and the vicar said, 'Thank Paula for finding her in time.' That produced the sort of noise that is described in novels as a murmur of assent, and then Glenys started asking questions—what had Kitty taken, and so on."

"And Bill?"

"He looked no different from all the others."

"Did he say anything about Kitty's drugs?"

"Not until I asked him. I thought you would like me to do that. He said he hadn't the slightest idea what Kitty dosed herself with. She didn't confide in him, and he never went near her private sanctum."

"I don't believe that," put in Paula.

"Neither do I, and I more or less said so. I said, 'Bill, if you were really so afraid that Kitty was trying to poison you, you'd want to know what sort of drugs she'd got upstairs.' "

Paula smiled. "Darling James! I couldn't have done it better myself. What did that provoke?"

"Horror all round. Pestering the poor man at a moment like this. Even the vicar gave me a dirty look. And as for Glenys— So, of course, I had to apologise, and we were just about settling down again when Roger Aston came in and went for Bill, as I told you."

James gave a great yawn.

"I don't believe you've slept," said Paula accusingly.

"Well," began James, and yawned again.

Paula waited.

"Okay," he said at last. "It's all your fault. You and your amateur sleuthing. You've got me hooked too. It's no crime nowadays, attempted suicide, but it did seem to me that none of Kitty's possessions ought to be touched until somebody in authority had had a look at them, so after the others had gone I told Bill I was going to sleep up in Kitty's room."

"Did you tell him why?"

"No. I only said I didn't want to disturb you and I had a fancy to sleep up there."

"Was he annoyed?"

"If he was, he didn't show it. He just looked at me as if I was crazy and said he was going to bed and would take the sleeping tablets that Dr. Shore left him."

"So he had them all the time."

"Yes. I was rather silly about that. I thought the vicar had taken them. Let's forget it. Something much more important. Of course I hardly slept. I was messing around for ages upstairs. And I found where she kept her pills. No wonder you and the doctor couldn't find them. D'you want to come and see?"

"Yes, please. Are you sure Bill's asleep? Not just pretending?"

"I'll check again."

James returned from Bill's bedroom to say that nobody who was only pretending to be asleep would lie with his mouth open, snoring, in quite so undignified a manner. When they reached the top landing, James did not go into Kitty's room, but signed to Paula to open the door next to the bathroom.

"I didn't go in there," said Paula. "I thought it was another bedroom. The latch seems very stiff. Are you sure it's not locked?"

"Try again."

Paula tried, and this time the handle turned.

The room was actually rather larger than Kitty's office, and it was crammed with trunks, suitcases, rolls of carpet, chairs that needed repair, and similar items that had no place in an orderly household, but that might be made use of some time.

James went straight to the filing cabinet that stood in the corner of the room nearest to the door. It was an old-fashioned steel cabinet, similar to the one in Kitty's room, containing three deep drawers wide enough to take foolscap-sized folders.

"Locked?" said Paula.

"The lock's broken. It's like those beastly things we used to have in the office at college."

"The drawers get stuck."

"Or else they shoot out suddenly and hit you in the solar plexus." James pulled at the top drawer with care. It appeared to be crammed with old files.

"Right at the back," he said. "See for yourself."

Paula saw and felt. At the far end of the drawer, separated from the files by the metal spring that held them upright, she found a little collection of boxes and bottles, a syringe, a thermometer, a nasal spray, and several other items.

"A miniature chemist's shop," she said.

"I'm going to phone Dr. Shore," said James, "and make sure she sees this lot before anybody else does. Do you approve?"

"Yes indeed."

"And then I'm going to have a bath. Up here in Kitty's bathroom, if you don't mind taking over the job of watchdog until the doctor arrives, and after that, what do you say to handing the whole thing over to Marilyn Shore and taking ourselves back to London for a bit of Sunday peace?"

Paula did not immediately reply.

"Or are you terribly keen to watch developments?" went on

James. "I've got a seminar first thing tomorrow morning, but I suppose we could stay here till this afternoon—if Glenys doesn't turn us out."

"We'll go as soon as we can," said Paula decisively. "I'm teaching tomorrow morning too. And we certainly shan't be wanted here. And there's no more snow."

But after James had spoken to the doctor, and while he was having his bath and Paula was drinking fresh tea that she had made in Kitty's room, she sat and thought about it and decided that she could not wash the Whitelands events out of her mind as easily as all that.

When James returned, she said, "I'd like to keep in touch with developments. We can always phone the hospital to ask about Kitty, but after she comes out—" She paused. "Which of all these people do you think is most likely to be telling the truth?"

"Certainly not Bill, although I don't need to make an excuse for calling him. We're still supposed to be friends. You don't trust Philip?"

"I don't know. He's supposed to be pro-Kitty, but after all he did leave her alone up there."

James groaned. "Darling Paula, please don't start again. Save it for Dr. Shore. Tell her all your suspicions and let her cope. She's a tough nut. She'll handle it."

"And we really don't know the Gravertons well enough," went on Paula, taking no notice of him. "Nor the vicar and his sister. We can't call up any of these people to ask if Bill is trying to poison Kitty or Kitty trying to poison him. But I've simply got to know what goes on here, James."

"There's the bell. It must be Marilyn. She's got here quickly. I'll let her in."

Dr. Shore looked as bright and energetic as ever, and was very grateful to be told about what James called the "drug haul."

"I'll take them," she said, accepting the offer of a cardboard container from among the junk in the spare room, "and I'll have a chat with Mrs. Burden when she is well enough. I'm going to suggest that she see a psychiatrist. How is Professor Burden?" she asked as they came downstairs again.

"Still sleeping off the pills you left him," replied James.

"Or pretending to," put in Paula.

"Pretending to?"

Dr. Shore looked at her in surprise.

"Paula thinks his sickness yesterday was all an act designed to drive his wife to distraction so that it would look as if she'd killed herself," explained James, "when in fact he'd done her in."

"Oh. That's interesting."

Dr. Shore stood holding the cardboard box under her arm and looked straight at Paula. "Any evidence?"

"None whatever, I'm afraid. Just my speculations and my observation of the parties concerned. And a very strong gut feeling that Kitty would never try to kill herself while her daughter was alive."

They surveyed each other for a moment or two, eyes almost on a level, Paula's blue and the young doctor's dark brown.

"That's my feeling too," said Marilyn at last. "Mrs. Burden was still too weak to talk much when I saw her early this morning, but she said she had no intention of committing suicide. She admits that she needed a knockout dose, and she said she had taken a couple of mild sleeping-tablets with some whisky. It had always worked on previous similar occasions."

"Then what—"

"I suspect that the analysis of the stomach contents may tell a somewhat different story," said Dr. Shore.

Paula found herself feeling quite weak. She was still holding tightly to her theory of what had happened, but the first hint that there might perhaps be some truth in it was turning out to be more alarming than gratifying.

"I've every intention of getting to the bottom of this business," said Dr. Shore, looking at Paula with some understanding, "and of course, we must remember that Mrs. Burden may not be telling the truth. Will you be staying here today?"

"Only for another hour or two," replied James. "Miss Fulham
—that's the vicar's sister, you may remember her from last night
—is coming over to look after Professor Burden if he needs it.
Paula and I have to get back to work tomorrow."

"You've got my phone number." Dr. Shore turned to Paula.
"I'll be in this evening if you'd care to call me."

"And here is mine," said Paula. "I feel rather responsible
towards Kitty Burden. If there's anything I can do to help—"

"You've saved her life," said Marilyn Shore with a faint smile.
"Let's hope it won't be necessary to repeat that service. Goodbye. Good luck."

They stood at the front door of The Twitten to watch her go.
It was still a very white world, but the sky was clear and the air
was crisp and still. Dr. Shore turned her car round with a great
crunching of the hard, uneven snow and drove off down Boyds
Lane. A postman was coming up the village street. James and
Paula came down the path to meet him and received a pile of
mail.

"What's it like this morning?" asked James.

"Could be worse," was the reply. "They're clearing the end
of the road. Boyds'll be able to shut their gates again."

"Awkward, isn't it," said James, "having only the private road
for access when there's a heavy snowfall."

"You can say that again," replied the postman. "Con-ser-va-
tion-ists!" The emphasising of each syllable made it sound like a
dirty word. "If they'd only stop trying to hang on to what
they've got, we might have a half-way decent society."

"Or it might be even worse than it is now," said James mildly.

The postman grunted and trudged off in the direction of the
vicarage.

"Local feuds again," commented Paula as they returned to the
house. "If I lived here—which heaven forbid—I should most
definitely be on the same side as the postman."

"He'll win in the end. Come on. I better go and take some tea
to Bill."

7

An hour later they were saying goodbye to Glenys. Bill had not yet got up.

"I think he's sulking," said Glenys, coming downstairs into the hall. "He hasn't forgiven you, James, for saying he must have known about Kitty's drug store."

"Don't you think he knew about it?"

"Of course he did. He's probably helped himself from it before now. But if you're thinking he deliberately switched some of the tablets from one bottle to another—no, that I don't believe. You were thinking that, weren't you?"

She turned from one to the other of them, a faint smile upon her face, the soft voice as calm and as pleasing as ever.

Paula and James exchanged glances. "Yes, we had thought it possible," said Paula. "If Kitty didn't deliberately take the wrong pills, then somebody else must have been tampering with them."

"Kitty took the wrong pills herself," said Glenys. "Whether intentionally or not, we shall probably never know."

"She says she didn't."

"She would obviously say that. Some women would revel in the position of being driven to suicide by their troubles. The martyr complex. But not Kitty. She can't endure to be in the position of victim. She always has to be in control, must always be in the right."

"You don't like her?"

Paula did not realise how accusing her voice sounded when she asked this question.

"Is that a crime?" countered Glenys, again with a faint smile.

"I'm sorry," said Paula quickly. "It's not my business. We'd better go."

"Are you sure I can't fill you a thermos flask? You might be glad of it if you get held up anywhere."

"No, thanks. We want to get back to London as soon as possible. The travel news said that the roads were all clear."

James had already been out to brush the snow off the Renault and to make sure that the car would start. As he turned it round, Paula said, "Boyds Lane? Or do we hope they've finished clearing the road by now?"

"Boyds, I think. I don't want to have to come all the way back if we can't get through."

As they drove through the open gateway into the farm road, Paula said, "I wonder if we will ever come back to Whitelands."

"As far as I'm concerned," said James, bumping over the deep frozen ruts, "I'll be delighted never to see the place again."

A few yards further on, Paula said, "I'm going to ask Kitty if she'd like to spend a few days in London when she leaves hospital."

"Why not? You do that."

"That'll keep her away from Bill for a little longer, and maybe I can persuade her to—"

"Damn," said James, not listening to her. "There's Roger the Viking. We're going to have to stop and talk to him."

Indeed, they had no choice. He stood in the middle of the road, a very tall figure with white hair and a very red face, dressed in ancient corduroy trousers and an equally battered brown leather jacket and brandishing a walking stick in his right hand.

James got out of the Renault and came towards him.

"They've cleared the road," shouted the old man. "We're going to shut our gates."

"Do you want me to turn back?" shouted James.

Roger Aston appeared to recognise him. He shifted the stick to his left hand, stepped forward, and shook hands with James.

"I know you, don't I? Come on. Come on in. Don't worry about the car. Leave it here. Mike!"

A stocky old man about two-thirds of Roger's height appeared from behind the hedge, accompanied by two bounding sheep-dogs.

"If you'll go and shut the west gate," said Roger comparatively quietly, "then nobody can get in."

"Aye, aye, sir."

The short man grinned, looked at them all from startlingly blue eyes, and hurried off down the track.

"Not very bright," said Roger Aston, poking a huge forefinger to the side of his head. "Lived in Boyds Cottage all his life. Can't turn him out. Does a few jobs for us. Looks after the dogs. Don't keep any sheep now. Let out most of the land. Keep an eye on 'em though." He chuckled. "Give 'em a bit of a fright now and then. Come on."

They followed him along a few more yards of the lane to where it turned sharply left and downhill towards the main road. On the right was the house, a beautifully proportioned flint building with white-painted window frames and a porch surmounted by a half-circle of fanlight. It was backed by conifers, and the stretch of garden in front included a frozen pond and a weeping willow tree.

"I'll go ahead and tell Phil," said Roger as they came to the gate. "Come in and get warm."

But James and Paula lingered for a moment on the doorstep. "You would think," murmured Paula, "that he would be all on the side of the road-improvers. It must be very annoying to have all the Whitelands traffic coming past the front door whenever it snows."

"Maybe he likes it. Maybe he gets lonely."

"It's a gorgeous house. But it's not being looked after," added Paula as they came into the entrance hall. This was high and square, with moulded ceilings and a fine open fireplace opposite the entrance. Over the fireplace was a gilt-framed mirror, blackened and cracked. There were some worn sheepskin rugs on the stone-flagged floor, and the whole place felt very damp and chilly.

"No wonder Philip worries about the heating," said Paula.

"Roger is supposed to be very rich but very mean," said James, "but I wonder—"

He was interrupted by the boom of Roger's voice.

"Come on. This way. Coffee in the breakfast-room. Phil's just finishing his breakfast."

The door they went through led into a passage with a rather lower ceiling than that of the hall and at the far end of it there was warmth. Philip was sitting at a huge mahogany table that had been pushed right into the far corner of the room under the window. He had his back to them, and in front of him was a tray on which stood a jar of marmalade, some slices of bread propped up against it, butter still in its foil wrapping, and a cup the size of a soup bowl.

He got up from the table when they came forward; he looked rather embarrassed and he frowned at his father, who took no notice at all.

"I'm afraid you won't find any gracious living at Boyds," he said. "We are no longer geared to receiving visitors, but if you can find yourselves somewhere to sit, I'll fetch some more coffee."

Apart from the table and some dining-chairs with upholstered seats which were shedding their stuffing, the room seemed to be bare of furniture. But the blue-and-red Persian carpet was in good condition, and the gas-heater that was fitted into the marble fireplace gave a welcome glow and adequate warmth.

Roger followed Philip out of the room, leaving the door open.

"I'm sorry, Phil," they heard him say. "Oughtn't I to have asked them in?"

"It doesn't matter, I suppose," came the reply in tones that were a mixture of annoyance and resignation.

"I'll do the coffee."

"No, Pater, you never put enough in."

Paula and James drew their chairs closer to the gas fire and smiled at each other. After the tense unhappiness of the Burdens' household, the crumbling grandeur of Boyds was really rather restful. In spite of the surface irritation, there was plainly genuine affection between the Astons, father and son.

They returned to the breakfast-room, Roger carrying the tray and Philip watching him anxiously. I shall never again be able to think of Philip Aston as just a slick and arrogant city lawyer, said Paula to herself; how little we know of people until we see them on their home ground.

The coffee, which turned out to be excellent, was poured into blue-and-gold cups that looked as if they had come out of the Victoria and Albert Museum. The biscuits, which were very stale, were offered by Roger on a cracked white plate that had grimy patches around the edge.

Paula took one and let it lie on her saucer. She smiled at the old man and thanked him, and then she suddenly felt rather shy. A memory from early childhood had flashed into her mind. She had been staying in the country with her grandparents, and they had called at the great house of the village.

Of course, they had gone to the tradesmen's entrance—her grandparents had a small market garden—but for some reason or other they had been taken into one of the big reception-rooms. Paula had clung to her elder sister's hand, but Stella had been trembling too. There had been a great white fireplace, a shining brass poker and coal scuttle, and a small table made of different-coloured bits of wood. The young Paula could only just see the top of it. Then a man's voice, loud but not unfriendly, had asked if the children would like some orange juice, and after that something awful had happened. Perhaps Paula had spilt the juice.

At that point memory faded. But some hurt or embarrassment or guilt had remained buried for years, so that Paula Glenning, Ph.D., scholar and teacher and author of a successful biography, felt herself momentarily ill at ease and was glad to let James do the talking.

James Goff was never ill at ease. But of course, Paula reminded herself, he came from the same sort of social background as the owners of Boyds. One didn't notice it most of the time. With people like James, the upper-class origins had become very much overlaid by the successful professional and the money-maker. It showed only when one stepped back into the past, into a social order that had gone for ever.

James was talking about the portrait that hung over the fireplace—the only picture left in the room, although the marks on the wallpaper showed that others had once hung there. The portrait was of a young woman in uniform, the pale blue of the Royal Air Force. She had large, dark, liquid eyes and a full and rather sulky-looking mouth—by no means a typical English society beauty.

"My mother," said Philip. "She was half-Maltese. I'm supposed to be like her. She died when I was ten."

"And you've no brothers or sisters?" asked Paula.

Philip shook his head and smiled. "The family is dying out. I've nothing but a failed marriage and no children."

Roger, who had been sitting brooding with his elbows resting on the table and his chin cupped in his hand, suddenly broke into violent speech.

"That can be remedied, sir! And must be remedied."

For a moment they glared at each other, father and son. Paula's thoughts flew to Kitty. How old was she? Thirty-seven? Not too old. But she and Philip had better hurry up. And what about Bill? A legitimate grandchild was what Roger wanted. Wasn't that a very good motive for getting Bill out of the way?

"Have you any more news of Kitty?" James was asking.

"I called the hospital just before you came," replied Philip. "She's doing very well."

"Nice gal," Roger was muttering, staring at the table again. "Good-looking. Clever."

"But what about Bill?" asked James bluntly.

"She won't leave him," said Philip, forestalling another explosion from his father, "because he won't pay for Marie if she does. There'd have to be a divorce settlement, of course, but it wouldn't be enough."

"But couldn't you—" began Paula. She wanted to ask, "Couldn't you and your father help her with Marie?" but thought better of it. James could get away with asking impertinent questions, but it wouldn't do for her to try it. Besides, she was beginning to think that it really must be shortage of money, and not meanness, that accounted for the state of the house. It could well be that Philip, knowing how much the house meant to his father, was spending much of his own income on keeping it going somehow. It could be that they were seriously in debt. Was it really a grandchild that Roger wanted from Kitty? Or was it a rich wife for his son?

But Kitty had no money of her own. The only way she could become rich was if Bill were to die, leaving her his estate.

"Scandalous, disgraceful, ought not to be allowed," Roger was muttering. "Nice woman like that tied to such a monster. You ought to do something about it, Phil."

"Such as what, Pater?"

"Take her to London with you. Make her come and stay here." The old man, slumped in a chair beside the table, was looking less vigorous than he had previously, and his voice became more and more despondent as he continued talking, more to himself than to the others.

"Kitty. Pretty little Kitty. To have a woman in the house again. But she'd find it too rough. Not comfortable enough for her. Eh?"

The question seemed to be addressed to Paula. "I don't think

Kitty would mind at all," said Paula, pleased with the idea of Kitty coping with Boyds.

"She won't come," said Philip. "I've told you why."

"Marie," said Roger in his hopeless voice. And then his mood suddenly changed again, and he straightened himself up and banged a fist on the table, so that the tray with the cups and saucers shook. "How long is the poor little beast going to live?"

Ah, thank God, thought Paula, at last somebody actually voices the thought that is in all our minds but we are too squeamish to speak, too civilised, too insistent on the right of every individual to live out its natural life, whatever the effect on others.

Philip roused himself to answer. "Nobody knows. Obviously she's not going to survive into old age, but with the sort of care she's getting, it could be quiet a number of years."

"That's no good," said Roger. "Kitty will be too old. And I'll be dead. Phil." His voice was wheedling now; he was playing the pathetic old man. "I wish you'd let me talk to her."

"I'm not stopping you. It won't make any difference."

Philip turned to Paula. "Would you like some more coffee?"

It was the signal for them to go. Philip had not wanted their visit at all, but he had humoured his father.

James got to his feet. "Do you want us to drive back to the village," he asked Roger, "or may we continue along your road until we join the main road?"

"Gate's shut," said Roger, "but I'll come and open it for you."

James began to protest that there was no need, but the old man was determined to come, and he insisted on trudging along in the ruts of snow in front of the car, so that James, swearing softly, was obliged to bump and skid along in bottom gear.

"He wants to tell us something," murmured Paula.

They reached the gate. The snow around it had been cleared, and Roger pulled the gate open. Then he came up to the car, and Paula wound down the window and leaned out.

"Thank you for the coffee," she said. "I loved seeing Boyds, and I hope you will have your wish."

"Thank you. What d'you think of my son?"

Paula thought quickly. "I think he's devoted to you and you to him."

"And Kitty? D'you think he really means to marry Kitty?" The old man's voice sounded puzzled and anxious. "Phil's a strange boy. Like his mother. You don't always know what he's thinking."

"I don't really know either of them well enough to answer that," said Paula carefully. "They certainly seem very close, but what about other women in his life?"

"Other women? I don't know. He never tells me. I don't know anything about his life in London. But I don't think there's anybody else. He's like me. He's a one-woman man. Once it was his mother. Then his wife."

A pause.

"What went wrong?" asked Paula at last.

"He never told me. I've sometimes wondered whether it was my fault."

The pathetic act again, thought Paula, but she could well imagine that a wife of Philip's might have felt herself in competition with the old man and that the resulting strains could lead to a breakup of the marriage. It was not everybody who could cope with Roger.

"You get on well with Kitty?" she asked him.

"I've always thought so, but of course, she doesn't know—"

Another pause. James appeared to be about to break the silence, and Paula gave him quite a sharp kick on the ankle. He subsided, wincing and grumbling.

Paula was just about to prompt the old man when he spoke again. "It's not only the grandson. It's the money to keep Boyds going. Phil's done his best, and we've sold some of the best pieces, but as you can see—"

James leaned across Paula, determined to have his say, and

spoke to Roger. "It's a historic house. How about the National Trust? Or English Heritage? Wouldn't they help you?"

Roger Aston's face became redder and redder. He raised his stick in a threatening manner and looked as if he was about to explode.

"Never, never!" His arm came down again. "Never," he repeated more calmly. "Boyds is mine and it stays mine till I die."

"Of course it does," said Paula soothingly. "I am sure you will find an answer to your problem."

The car was moving before she had finished speaking: James had had enough.

"Goodbye!" Paula called back to Roger as they waited to turn onto the main road.

She saw him shut the gate and stand leaning against it, a big, tall figure against the white of the field beyond, protecting his own against all comers.

"That one," said James as they filtered into the traffic and joined the outside world again, "is barely half-way sane. He wouldn't stop at murder to get what he wants."

"Poor Philip," said Paula. "I don't think I should ever come to like him, but all the same, poor Philip."

8

Dr. Shore kept her promise and telephoned Paula about half past eight that evening.

James had long since departed for his own apartment. They had discussed the Whitelands affair ad nauseam during the drive back to London and over lunch in their favourite Hampstead pub, and both of them were glad to return to scholarship and solitude. For once James failed to make his little speech about how nice it would be if they bought a house together, which was a relief to Paula because he had been talking about it more and more recently, and she felt sure that it would ruin their good fellowship if they were always together.

The twenty-four hours' close-range view of the marriage of Bill and Kitty Burden had deeply disturbed them both. The glimpse into the Aston household, while comforting in that it revealed genuine affection, had done nothing to remove the overall impression: marriage and family relationships were the very devil; think very long and carefully before giving up your precious freedom.

Paula was rereading portions of *Ulysses,* a book which she rather disliked, and included from duty, not from inclination, in her twentieth-century literature course, when the phone rang and Marilyn Shore announced herself.

"Mrs. Burden is fine. She's going to a convalescent home to-morrow for a few days. Actually she would be well enough to go home, but in the circumstances—"

"Oh, don't let her go home!"

"I can't stop her if she insists."

"I suppose not. May I have the address?"

"The convalescent home? That's why I'm calling."

Paula noted it. "That can't be far from where Marie is," she commented.

"Mrs. Burden chose it for that reason."

The doctor's voice was non-committal.

"Did you find out anything more about the drugs?" asked Paula.

"No progress at all. Mrs. Burden swears she took her usual mild tranquillisers. Professor Burden swears he knew nothing of the drugs in the filing cabinet."

"So what happens? Do you give her them back?"

"Some of them. I have no authority over her. I can only advise. She has no illegal drug in her possession and swears that they have all been legitimately obtained on prescription, except for the diomorphine, which she admits getting through a nursing acquaintance, whose name she won't give."

"But that was what she was going to give Marie," said Paula.

"Exactly. And I'm not handing it back to her. Although she'll probably get hold of some more if she wants to."

"Dr. Shore—Marilyn—do you think that Kitty Burden is a danger to herself or to others?"

"If you really want my opinion, yes, I do, in her present circumstances. She is quite obsessional, quite beyond reason, about that child."

"Will she try another mercy killing—if one can call it that?"

"I've warned Mrs. Matthews and I've warned the convalescent home, but on the whole I don't think that is likely to happen again. She is only too aware that if she tried it, she would lose access to Marie. That's what really scares her, and that is how I have persuaded her to see a psychiatrist."

"In Sussex?"

"No. In London. Friday morning at the North London Clinic."

"That's only a few minutes away from me. That settles it. I'm going to get Kitty Burden to stay with me on Friday night and over the weekend. Would you back me up?"

"I most certainly will."

The doctor was just about to ring off when Paula asked, "If you think you've scared her off attacking Marie, what are you afraid she might do?"

"Your guess is as good as mine. You've seen how things stand in that household, and she seems determined to go back to her husband. Perhaps you will be able to talk some sense into her. Goodbye."

Paula replaced the phone. The copy of *Ulysses* still lay open on her lap. She glanced down at it and read a few sentences, but the Dublin of 1904 seemed as remote as prehistory. She put the book aside and turned to some of the D. H. Lawrence short stories, also on the reading list of her Monday-morning class, but these, too, failed to compete with the real-life drama that had been taking place fifty miles south of London.

Again and again, during the following days, Paula's thoughts reverted to the inhabitants of Whitelands. Students found her less enthusiastic than usual in her teaching, and on the weekly visit to her sister, her young niece and nephew openly accused her of not listening to the tale of their adventures in their new school. Her sister and brother-in-law, after the children had gone to bed, exchanged looks of amusement and said, "Out with it, Paula. Tell us about the current mystery."

"There's nothing special," protested Paula. "Only some marriage problems of a friend of James's."

"Who has murdered whom?" asked Stella.

"Nobody yet."

"Then who is going to?" put in Don.

"Do you really want to hear about it? I don't want to bore you."

They burst out laughing. "I'd far rather listen to your exploits," said her brother-in-law, "then watch the current run of television programmes. They are abysmal."

Paula embarked on a carefully edited version of the events of last weekend. Donald was an engineer; her sister, Stella, a teacher. They were her nearest and dearest; their house in a North London suburb was a centre of stability for her own life, very precious to her. But their opinions and their outlook on life were so very different from her own that she always rearranged her thoughts when she was with them, never giving any hint of the loneliness and depression that attacked her so savagely from time to time. Any such admission would bring on a joint attack from Stella and Don: she must marry James. That, in their opinion, was the solution to the problem of Paula.

Of course, there would be ups and downs: that was what marriage was about, wasn't it? You had to take the rough with the smooth. Etc., etc.

It was Don who talked like this, always in clichés. This minor irritation, plus the keeper failing of a certain lack of generosity, had in the past driven Stella to pour out her regrets by the hour to her sister. But those days seemed to be over. Either Don had improved or Stella had grown more tolerant now that the children were at school and she herself in a full-time job again. This was fine, except that it meant that they had a tendency to join forces in attacking Paula.

To tell them about the disastrous marriage of Bill and Kitty Burden would be to resurrect all the old familiar arguments. Kitty would be condemned outright, and Paula, half-agreeing with them in her heart, would find herself springing all the more fervently to Kitty's defence.

How to tell the story but avoid an argument?

"D'you remember that time we were taken to the manor-house?" Paula suddenly asked her sister. "With Gran and Granpa?"

"Yes." Stella looked rather surprised. "You were fascinated by the chess-board top of the games table. You wanted to know whether the different coloured bits of wood were all the same level, and you put your sticky fingers all over it."

"Oh. Was that what I did? I knew it was something dreadful, but I couldn't remember what."

"Just like Paula." Don regarded them both indulgently. "Incorrigibly inquisitive. Even at that age."

"I suddenly remembered it," said Paula hurriedly, "when we were invited into the Great House at Whitelands."

Her story rolled on from there. Roger Aston, proud and impoverished and craving a grandchild, with Kitty Burden as the answer to his prayer. This was the way to introduce Kitty, as the woman plotted against, not as the plotter.

Paula could tell a story well, once she had made up her mind which aspect to emphasise. At one point Stella interrupted her.

"Just a moment. Let me recap. You've got Roger Aston and his son, Philip, desperate to restore the family fortunes through Philip's marriage. Couldn't they find a better candidate than Kitty Burden? No, Paula, let me go on. Let's take Kitty's pros and cons. She's pretty and very competent, and she's just young enough to produce a grandchild. And Philip loves her. Yes?"

"Yes. That's one thing I'm fairly sure of."

"Okay. Those are the certainties. Not much to bank on when you think of the mountains of uncertainties. Kitty's got a husband who doesn't look like dying for a long time—at any rate, not from natural causes. Kitty's also got a Down's syndrome daughter who won't die just yet either and is an enormous financial drain. For Roger and Philip to get what they want, first of all the husband has to die; you've agreed that Kitty's not going to get much money if he doesn't. After that, the daughter has to die, because however large a fortune Professor Burden leaves to Kitty, it's hardly likely to be enough to keep both the daughter and the Great House going—not to mention any grandchildren —in the style that Roger would consider suitable."

"You're right," said Paula. "I don't think Roger has much money sense. Pride takes precedence over reasonable economy."

"I know I'm right. Kitty's a rotten proposition moneywise.

And in other ways as well. How does she feel about it herself? Supposing she's got rid of Bill and inherited his money. She must have had that possibility in mind when she married him. That leaves her with enough to keep her daughter and to enjoy her own freedom. A very nice position indeed. Why on earth should she marry Philip and take on his father and all his illusions as well? Just tell me why, Paula."

Stella, ignoring her husband's protests, threw a cigarette at her sister and took one for herself.

"Thanks," said Paula. "Sorry, Don. We'll just have this one cig. No more. No reason at all why Kitty should marry Philip. Unless she loves him so devotedly that—"

"Does she love him so devotedly?"

Stella was enjoying herself. Ever since childhood she had been used to feeling intellectually rather inferior to her younger and brighter sister, but this time, for once, she was getting the better of a discussion.

Paula began to laugh. "I can't say I've seen much sign of it," she admitted. "Okay, Stella. You win. Kitty is just making use of Philip. That's your next point, isn't it?"

"You've said it," said Stella cheerfully. "I'm sure Philip suspects it, even if his father doesn't."

"I think Roger has his doubts too," said Paula, remembering her final conversation with the old man before leaving Whitelands. "In fact, I'm beginning to think that my whole idea of a plot to get hold of Kitty to rescue Boyds is a non-starter."

"There probably has been such a scheme," said Stella kindly, "in Roger's mind, if not in anybody else's. But in any case, it wasn't Kitty's husband who nearly died. It was Kitty herself. What do you make of that?"

Paula did not immediately answer. Don, getting up to refill their coffee cups, said, "She sounds thoroughly neurotic to me. Marrying a man she doesn't care for in the least in order to keep a vegetable daughter in luxury. It's crazy. And it's not fair on the husband."

"I think she's been doing her best," said Paula rather doubt-fully.

"Oh, sure. That's just what a man wants for a wife, isn't it? An agonised martyr, silently telling everybody what hell her life is and what a bastard he is."

Paula bit back a sharp retort and made a mental note to ask James whether this was how he saw it.

"Could you feel that way," she said, turning to Stella, "about a severely brain-damaged child?"

"Up to a point I can understand," replied her sister thought-fully. "I think I might feel that it was somehow my fault and that I'd got to pay for it. But I don't think I'd feel that I had to make everybody else pay for it too, which is what Kitty seems to be doing. It's easy to talk, though, when one isn't in that position. Thank heaven. But I can understand her getting desperate and trying to overdose the child. Poor woman."

"And then overdosing herself."

Paula put this as a statement of fact, not as a question. She was interested to hear Stella's response. If it was straightforward, then she would not mention her own suspicions of Bill.

"Oh, yes indeed," said Stella. "I can understand that too. What on earth must she be feeling now? It hardly bears thinking of."

"She's coming up to London tomorrow," said Paula, "to see one of the psychiatrists at the North London Clinic. And then she's staying with me for the weekend."

Both her hearers looked rather alarmed.

"Do take care, Paula," said Stella anxiously.

"You'd better check her suitcase for syringes and pills," said Don, only half-joking.

"I'm fetching her from the clinic," replied Paula, "and I shall take their advice."

The North London Clinic was a stark square concrete building breaking up a row of mellow brick houses in a tree-lined street.

It had been built at the end of World War II and had retained an air of austerity both without and within, in spite of newly painted walls and pleasant landscape pictures and plenty of comfortable chairs.

Paula sat in the waiting-room opposite an anxious-looking middle-aged couple talking in semi-whispers about their son. Drugs and depression. It sounded a very familiar story to somebody whose work was with eighteen- to twenty-year-olds. Trying not to hear, Paula picked up a copy of a glossy magazine, which fell open at the problems page, and she found herself reading, "My wife and I have been happily married for twenty-five years and have three lovely children. Now she says she wants to leave home and train as a computer-programmer. How can I make her see that this is ridiculous at her age?"

Paula smiled to herself as she turned to the answer, but she had no time to read it. A quite girlish young West Indian woman was standing in front of her, looking both elegant and rather odd in a heather-coloured blouse and skirt.

"Are you waiting for Mrs. Burden?" she asked in a voice which matched her costume.

Paula stood up. The woman introduced herself as Dr. Latham. As they walked together into the foyer, she said, "Mrs. Burden is coming to see me again next Friday. I hope we shall be able to help her."

"Is she going home?" asked Paula.

"That's what she seems to want."

"But she oughtn't to— I mean, it isn't safe. What about her pills?"

The West Indian, who really looked absurdly young to be in charge of such a case, younger even than Dr. Shore, raised her eyebrows slightly.

"She has been prescribed an antidepressant and a narcotic. She knows the correct dose."

Paula subsided. After all, what could any of them do? Kitty could no longer be described as an emergency, and in any case, the pressure on hospitals was such that they were having to turn away even emergencies much of the time. She realised then that her disappointment was due to some lingering illusions of her own. Some part of her was still living in a bygone world, or maybe a world that had never been, where doctors were old and wise and reassuring, not young and smart and realistic.

"We have to hope that she will not make another attempt," said Dr. Latham. "We have to hope," she repeated with a slight forward movement of the head and an emphasis on the world 'hope.'

Paula felt a little better. "I'm going to try to persuade her not to return to her husband," she said.

The young woman smiled faintly. "Perhaps you will be more successful than we have been. Good luck. Here she comes."

Paula had been telling herself that she must expect to find Kitty altered, but nevertheless she was shocked when she saw her. There seemed to be no connection between the lovely and elegant hostess of the lunch party at Whitelands and the thin, beaten-looking woman in an old tweed coat and clumsy boots. Her face was masklike, freshly made-up, and she stared at Paula as if she barely recognised her.

"Hullo, Kitty," said Paula much too brightly. "Shall I take your suitcase?"

Kitty yielded it up, and the freed hand began to make convulsive movements.

"I've got the car parked just up the road," said Paula.

They came out of the building into hazy winter sunshine and walked in silence the few yards up the hill.

"You're brave to drive in London," said Kitty as she got into the yellow mini.

"It took a lot of getting used to, and I'm still jittery at times."

"I shall never learn to drive. I ran into a child on my first lesson, and it put me off for ever."

"What happened?"

"Oh, the kid wasn't hurt, but the instructor went into hysterics. He hadn't braked in time. He'd been paying more attention to me than to my progress. Trying to fix a date. I was eighteen then and rather glamorous."

"What a pity," said Paula. "But, of course, it wasn't your fault."

"I know. But it was a very bad beginning. And it made me feel I wasn't to be trusted with a lethal weapon in my hands."

"Have you been talking about this to the doctor at the clinic?"

"Oh, yes. All the traumas. We've been sorting them all out to try to make a pretty pattern."

Paula, who had been feeling more and more disturbed, was somewhat relieved to hear this echo of Kitty's former sardonic self.

"We're in luck," she said a few minutes later. "There's a parking space in front of the house. I'm three floors up without a lift. Sorry."

Kitty trudged up the stairs behind her without speaking, but the masklike face broke into a smile as they came into Paula's ever untidy room. Then the smile faded, and when Paula asked if she would be comfortable sleeping on the sofa, Kitty sat down on it suddenly, buried her face in the cushions, and began to shake and writhe in a storm of tears.

Brandy? Coffee? thought Paula, and then, almost immediately afterwards, No, that's the easy way out. She needs comfort and love, and what does it matter if I'm snubbed or pushed aside?

So she sat down on the sofa beside Kitty and put her arms round her and gently turned her head round so that it rested on her shoulder, and gradually the trembling and the sobbing stopped. After a little while Kitty pulled herself away and said, "Where's the bathroom?"

When she came back, dry-eyed but with no fresh mask, she accepted a cup of tea and a sandwich and said, "I'm not going to keep on apologising. You must have known what you were letting yourself in for when you invited me."

"Of course I did," said Paula. "And I'll stop apologising too.

What's the matter with women? We're hopeless. All of us. Why should we always feel that we've got to apologise for the deficiencies of our housekeeping or for our displays of emotion? What is this extraordinary image of perfection that we are all the time mentally comparing ourselves with?"

Kitty actually laughed. It was not a happy laugh, but it was natural and unforced, and the bitterness was absent from her voice when she replied.

"That's what I used to wonder until I turned into one of the greatest offenders myself. But I've been punished for it. Do you want to know why I had that attack of hysterics the moment I came into your flat?"

Paula refilled her cup and waited.

"Envy," went on Kitty. "Sheer bloody envy. Here you are, in your snug little hidey-hole all of your own. You're warm and comfortable, and you've got some gorgeous books and some nice pictures, and you're not trying to keep up any appearances, and you've paid for it all through your own efforts, and you can do what you like. Envy. I'm absolutely eaten up with envy of you, Paula."

"Well, that certainly makes a change," said Paula. "Most of my friends and relations groan when they come to see me and want to know if I am ever going to move out of this slum and make myself a really nice little home."

"James too?"

"No. James wants us to marry and buy one of those incredibly expensive new town houses and live a beautifully cultured life together."

Kitty shuddered. "Don't. It wouldn't work."

"Of course it wouldn't. I think he's beginning to realise that himself after watching you and Bill last weekend."

Kitty looked very unhappy. "Oh, Paula. I'm so sorry."

"There you go again. I thought apologising was banned."

"Ah, but this is different. This isn't just lazy self-defence. I feel very distressed to think of the trouble that Bill and I have caused

to you and others as well. It is terrible how unhappiness spreads
out like the ripples when you throw a stone into a pond. Do you
remember what was said about the Carlyles' marriage? Well, of
course you do. You teach English literature."

"You mean, what a good thing it was that Thomas Carlyle
married Jane and so made only two people miserable instead of
four?"

"That's right. Except that it isn't right at all. A miserable marriage spreads its poison around."

"Then why don't you end it, Kitty?"

Paula had not meant to come to this point so soon, but the
opportunity was too good to miss.

Kitty did not reply. After a while she said, just as if Paula had
never asked the question, "I have friends in London whom I'd
like to visit. I've had very little chance to see them since I married Bill. What are your plans for the weekend?"

"Nothing in particular. There's some reading I have to do.
Why don't you make your arrangements, and then if there's any
time left, we could go to a theatre or a concert together."

Kitty thank her and collected the cups and plates.

"You've been making marmalade," she exclaimed as she carried them into the kitchen.

The line of glass jars still stood along the back of the table:
Paula had not got round to stowing them away.

"Yes," she said thoughtfully. "That's how it all began. It's
turned out rather well. The marmalade, I mean. Help yourself."

Kitty pulled the top of one of the jars and dipped a spoon in.
"Lovely. Paula, I've had an idea. How about you letting me
cook you a dinner? I can't think of anything that would give me
greater pleasure. Do say yes. This evening?"

There was no possible way to refuse, even if Paula had wanted
to, and there was also no possible way of reintroducing the subject of Kitty's marriage. The hours passed agreeably enough,
with some quite lively conversation, but Kitty avoided any discussion of her own affairs by the simple expedient of ignoring

any remarks of Paula's that might lead in that direction, and it was not until the Monday morning, when they were having a leisurely breakfast together, that they regained the degree of intimacy of that first hour.

9

It was Kitty who opened the subject.

"I want to thank you. I want to thank you in particular for not spoiling the whole weekend by talking about my problem. If you think I want to go back to Whitelands, you couldn't be more wrong. Being here in your flat has been like being let out of prison into fresh air. I feel so much better for it."

She did indeed look better. Her dark hair had regained something of its gloss, and her face, with very little make-up, and lost some of its rigidity. She looked pale and worried, and her restless hands still looked as if they could find relief only in action, but she no longer gave the appearance of somebody who is tipping over the edge of rational control.

"I'm glad you feel better," said Paula.

"And I'm going back to Bill. I know you think I oughtn't to. So did Dr. Shore. So do the people at the clinic. It's not just because of Marie and the money. In fact, I'm almost coming round to thinking that Marie would be better in some public institution. At least there would be less danger that I might try . . ."

Kitty's voice faded away. When she spoke again, it was with greater firmness.

"I shall never do anything like that again," she said. "If I feel myself going out of control, I'll get in touch with Dr. Shore or with the clinic. No. It's not just because of Marie. It's because I hate failure. I had a job to do for Bill and I failed. I've got to try again."

"But Kitty, he's intolerable."

"Not so bad as I've made him appear. Treated differently, he'd behave differently."

"Flattery and pretence? Oh, Kitty, you disappoint me."

"I used to do it when I was his secretary. It's not so very difficult. It's like humouring a child."

"But marriage is different. And after all that's happened. And in any case, is it fair on Philip?"

"On Philip?" Kitty looked genuinely surprised.

"Yes. Isn't he in love with you? Why should he go on indefinitely propping up this idiotic farce of you and Bill?"

"But Paula." Kitty looked upset. "It's not like that at all. There's nothing between Philip and me."

"You told me you were lovers."

"No. I can't have done. There's no question of it."

"You told me when we were up in your room after you had run away from your lunch party. You said that Bill was no problem sexually because his inclinations, which weren't very strong in any case, were towards other men and that you yourself had your—'friend,' I think, was the word you used. I can't remember at what point it became obvious that the 'friend' was Philip, but it most certainly did become obvious."

Kitty got up from the table and sat down on the sofa. Paula took the chair opposite, and for a moment or two they stared at each other in silence.

"You're never going to believe that I had no intention of misleading you," said Kitty at last.

"No, I don't think I am going to believe that," said Paula. "You know perfectly well that you wanted it to be thought that you and Philip were lovers."

"It was the easiest way out. It helped Philip, and it didn't trouble me one way or the other."

"Then perhaps you would kindly tell me what the truth of the matter is. If you are capable of recognising the truth," added Paula unkindly, unable any longer to control her own anger and resentment at being deceived.

"If you knew Philip's father," began Kitty.

"I do know Philip's father. I've been invited into his house."

"Then you will have seen what he is like and what problems Philip has with him. And you can imagine what life would be like for Philip if Roger knew that his son was bisexual and that that was the main reason why his marriage failed."

"I can indeed," said Paula, beginning to feel a little less angry with Kitty as she became annoyed with herself for not suspecting this.

"I doubt if Roger even knows that a man can be attracted to both sexes," went on Kitty. "And he would think of a male homosexual as a painted boy dressed in woman's clothes. He's never had the slightest suspicion about Philip, and that's how it has to remain. Phil really loves his father, but it's a dreadful strain, constantly pretending. Neither of us actually planned to make Roger believe that I was Philip's woman. It just happened, and it turned out to be a wonderful alibi for Philip. Here was a woman at the same time desirable and totally unavailable. Roger might grieve over Philip's choice, but he had to accept it as a fact."

Kitty's words rang true. Paula, hastily reviewing in her mind the events of the weekend at Whitelands, could find no flaw in them. Kitty as a cover-up for Philip. That made sense, and it explained something that had been subconsciously worrying her a lot and that her sister had put her finger on at once. Kitty and Philip, supposed to be lovers, had in fact given no evidence at all of such a relationship. There was obviously plenty of trust and goodwill, but nothing of any stronger feeling.

"Yes," she said aloud. "That I can understand. It was stupid of me not to realise before."

"You were being much too battered by me and Bill. It's not surprising that you didn't start wondering about Philip."

"And what about Bill? Is there a relationship between him and Philip? Or is that too neat?"

"No," sighed Kitty, "it's not too neat. It's all part of it. A sort of camouflage for them both. A classic triangle. Husband, wife, and wife's lover. Actually it is the wife who is the odd one out. Not that there is any actual relationship between Bill and Philip. It's a kind of romantic fantasy thing. They feed each other with dreams. They flatter each other. Beautiful Greek boys in the great age of Athens. It's a big kinky, but harmless."

"I see. And you don't resent it? You are content to have a public image of a femme fatale and a private reality that neither of them cares about you?"

"But they do care about me. Philip is the best friend I've ever had." For the first time since she had begun her story, Kitty sounded agitated. "He's like a brother to me. More than a brother. I can't let him down. If I leave Bill, Philip loses his alibi."

"So that's the real reason. Not Marie and the money."

Kitty held her head in her hands. "It's all bound up together now. There's just no way out of the tangle. I've got to go on somehow. I've got to make it work."

Paula said nothing. She handed Kitty a cigarette, and they smoked in silence for a few minutes.

Then she asked suddenly, "Have you a lover?"

"No."

Paula was very tempted to pursue this line of questioning, but decided that this was not the right moment. There would be no sense in putting Kitty on her guard again and destroying the trust that had been re-established between them. In any case, Kitty's revelation about Philip had put the Whitelands affair into quite a different perspective. It had shifted the lights, shown up the grey areas, and made a much more intelligible pattern out of the whole. Paula felt that she ought to examine this newly re-vealed pattern before setting out to explore a completely new area of the maze.

But there was another question which she could safely ask.

"What do you think of Glenys Fulham? She seems to have a very soothing effect on Bill."

"Glenys? Oh, yes, Robert's sister. Yes, Bill likes her. She's got his measure, and he doesn't feel threatened by her."

"I was thinking that she'd be a far more suitable wife for him than you are."

"That's quite a thought. It never occurred to me, but you could be right. If I could only shift Bill off onto Glenys."

Kitty pondered this for a little while.

"No, it wouldn't work," she said at last. "Bill will lap up sympathy like the cat with the cream, but if he buys himself a wife, then he wants her to look good as well."

She stood up. "I look dreadful at the moment. I'll have to do something about it when I get home. It's been heaven these last few days, slopping around as I used to do."

Paula got up too. She was driving Kitty to the tube station before going on to the college, and it was time they left.

"Would you like to come and stay again? Weekend after next?"

"I'd love to, but I don't think I'd better make a habit of it. Bill wouldn't like it."

"But if you're coming up to the clinic—"

"I'm coming next Friday, but I think that'll be the last time. There's not much point in it. I know only too well what's the matter with me."

"I hate to think of you going back into that set-up."

"I chose it with my eyes open."

"You chose Bill. You didn't choose the Philip Aston complication."

"That's true," admitted Kitty. "But you know, in a way it makes it easier."

She was clearing the table, stacking the breakfast plates.

"Don't bother about that. I'll wash up this evening," said Paula. "Kitty," she added as they were putting on their coats, "why has Bill been tormenting you? From what you say, it can't be because of Philip. Presumably they understand each other.

Why should he drive you into the state you were in last weekend?"

"Sheer bloody-mindedness and boredom, I suppose," replied Kitty, and that was all that Paula could get out of her.

Two days later she was telling James about this conversation. Neither of them were teaching that afternoon, and they had driven from the college to Kenwood House on Hampstead Heath, a pleasant little outing for a winter day. The café provided good soup and salads, and they could look at the pictures without the pressure of crowds of people and relax in eighteenth-century elegance.

After deciding, as she always did, that she preferred Gainsborough portraits to Turner landscapes, Paula suggested that they should walk on Hampstead Heath for a while. The sun was shining and a fresh fall of snow had brought a renewed brightness to the scene without being deep enough to make walking difficult.

They came out onto the terrace and turned, by unspoken consent, into the path that led round the lake.

"We don't come here often enough," said James. "We must come to one of the open-air concerts next summer."

"We always say that and we never do."

"I know, but that's one of the minor pleasures of life, isn't it, vaguely planning to do things that one never does."

"Maybe, but I rather think it's a sign of getting older."

"In twenty years time, when we are both coming up to retirement, we shall be walking by the lake at Kenwood and having exactly this conversation."

"Very likely."

They walked on in deep contentment.

"I want to tell you about Kitty Burden," said Paula presently.

James gave a groan. "I knew it was too good to last. Do I have to listen to it now?"

"You know you want to hear. Are you listening, James?"

James replied with an unencouraging sort of noise, but after a while he gave up pretending not to be interested, and interrupted Paula's narration with so many questions that they walked much further than they had intended and had to hurry back, anxious that the gates might have been locked on the car.

"Did you guess about Philip?" asked Paula, when they had retrieved the Renault.

"No. No suspicion. How naive we are. Yet another sign that we are well past our youth."

A few minutes later he said, "I saw Bill yesterday. At the Eighteen-Ninety Club."

"Good Lord! What were you doing in that reactionary stronghold?"

"I was invited. By one of those self-made money men of whom you so disapprove. Though what right have you, a self-made woman if ever there was one—"

"Oh, do shut up, James. Tell me about Bill Burden."

"Nothing much to tell. We hardly spoke. He was with a group of youngish people who seemed to be treating him with great respect. He looked very spry and was playing the elder statesman of economic theory for all he was worth."

"So not everybody agrees with you that he is an academic has-been."

"These people were not academics. You don't find scholars at that sort of club."

"Except yourself."

"And I'm a very poor scholar. Don't contradict. That's your opinion of me, and you've troubled to hide it during all the fifteen years we have known each other."

"Damn," said Paula, "we're getting back to ourselves again, and I want to know about Bill. He looked cheerful, did he?"

"Very much so. In his element."

"Did he mention Kitty?"

"I asked him about her, and he said that she had been to see a specialist, who had been most helpful and also most hopeful. A careful sort of reply, obviously for the benefit of his companions, who were listening, but I think he'd have said much the same even if we'd been alone."

"In other words, James darling, he was presenting exactly the sort of picture that he was before we went down to Whitelands."

"Exactly. Back to square one."

"And Kitty seems determined to keep it up. At least she was determined to when I last saw her."

"So there is absolutely nothing we can do about it, Paula, and it would be much the best if we could try to forget the whole business."

"It's you who dragged me into it in the first place," Paula reminded him, "and I can't forget it. Or rather, I can't forget Kitty. Sometimes I could weep for her, and at other times I'd like to strangle her; but whichever it is, I've got to know what happens to her."

"Maybe she'll now be able to keep up her act," said James as they joined the long line of cars waiting to filter down into Hampstead High Street.

"I hope so. No, I don't hope so," said Paula. "It's horrible. The whole set-up. I don't know what I hope. I only know that there are so many explosive possibilities down there in Sussex that something has to blow up some time or other."

"As long as I'm not in the middle of it," said James as the traffic moved on at last.

A couple of months later James reported that he had met Bill again, that he looked very well, and that, according to him, Kitty was completely recovered and very contented in her quiet life. She had taken up bird-watching and botanising, and was accompanying Henry Graverton on some of his excursions.

"I wonder what Louise thinks of that," commented Paula. "There's a bit of jealousy there, you know, James."

"There'll always be jealousy with Kitty around. And as far as I can remember, Louise Graverton was no beauty."

"Neither was Henry. But he was nice. I wonder—"

"Oh no, Paula. Please. Not another man in Kitty's life."

"But there is another man. She as good as told me. And I'm sure he's right there in Whitelands."

"Can't we just not think about them?"

"No. I can't. And neither can you. If you weren't still thinking about them, you wouldn't have told me that you'd seen Bill again."

"Then next time I run into him, I shan't tell you," retorted James irritably; but of course, he did, and the report was very much the same as before, except that this time Kitty had taken to going to church and was full of good works, constantly in consultation with the vicar and his sister.

"That sounds a bit safer," remarked Paula, "although I can't help wondering what she is really up to. Kitty, I mean. Why don't we go down to Brighton one weekend? We can be making a sort of mini–literary pilgrimage. The Woolf house at Rodmell and then Charleston Farmhouse, and being so near, we thought we might as well revisit Whitelands. What do you think, James?"

"I think it's a crazy idea."

But a little later he said, "At least it won't be snowing in June."

And a little later, "I wonder if Roger Aston is still alive. And I wonder whether they've started on those road-works."

After that, it didn't take very long for Paula to persuade him to fix a date.

10

At ten past six on a summer Friday morning, the day before the one decided on, Paula was awakened by the telephone ringing.

"Did you hear the news?"

James's voice sounded very excited. "Wake up," he went on in response to the mildly complaining noises that came over the wire. "Do try and wake up, Paula. Bill Burden is dead."

"What!"

"I thought that would grab you."

"Tell me. Quick!"

"I don't know much. It was a radio news item. Professor William Burden, the well-known economist, was found dead late yesterday evening at the bottom of a disused chalk quarry about a mile from his home in Sussex. Paula, are you still there?"

"Yes. I'm a bit shattered. Is foul play suspected?"

"They didn't say so."

"Suicide?"

"They didn't say anything more at all. Only that he leaves a widow. There may be a longer account in the papers."

"That's no good. I want to know now. I'm going to call Kitty."

"You can't do that at this hour."

Paula reluctantly agreed.

"Come and have breakfast with me," said James, "and then we'll phone her together."

Two hours later, and after half a dozen unanswered telephone calls to The Twitten, they decided that there was going to be no reply.

"She's either not there," said James, "or else she's heavily doped."

"Let's try Dr. Shore.

This time they were in luck.

"I'm glad you called," said Marilyn Shore. "I was thinking about you last night when I was with Mrs. Burden. She is staying at Boyds for the time being, in case you are wanting to get in touch with her. Philip Aston is there. Have you got the number?"

"Yes, thanks," replied Paula. "We'll try them later. But what happened? To Professor Burden, I mean."

"Mrs. Burden's story is that he had gone out for a walk after dinner. He often does on fine summer evenings, usually taking the path up the hill to see the sunset. Sometimes she goes with him, but last night there was a television play she wanted to watch. About half past ten, when it was quite dark, she began to be anxious. During the next half-hour she telephoned all their friends and acquaintances in the neighbourhood to ask if he had called in on them, and finally a search party was organised."

"What was in it?" asked Paula a trifle breathlessly.

"Philip Aston and his father, Mr. and Mrs. Graverton, and the vicar. They all of them know the area well. Mrs. Burden stayed at home in case her husband should turn up. It was Mrs. Graverton who actually found Professor Burden. About halfway up the hill path there is a favourite viewpoint at the top of an old chalk-pit. The edge of it is overgrown with gorse bushes, but there is a warning notice and a wire fence, which apparently is in need of repair. There have been one or two accidents to ramblers who didn't know the area, but everybody in Whitelands knows it well, and one would have to be drunk or ill or very careless to be in danger."

Marilyn Shore paused.

"Or suicidal," put in Paula, "or—"

"Yes," said Dr. Shore.

"Any evidence that he wasn't alone?"

"None at all."

"Police?"

"They're up there now. There is not much doubt about the spot where he fell. It's where the fence is broken. The earth is very dry and the chalk is crumbling."

"What do you think yourself?"

"I think that a coroner's inquest is going to record a verdict of accidental death, with some rather nasty comments about the state of the fence and the negligence of the local authority."

"But what do you *really* think?"

It was James who put this question after he had snatched the telephone from Paula.

"I've no opinion," said Dr. Shore. "Why don't you come down and decide for yourselves?"

"We're going to do just that," said James. He replaced the receiver and turned to Paula. "Shall we try to get hold of Philip? Or do you think it would be better just to turn up?"

"I'd rather just turn up," said Paula. "Philip might try to put us off."

"If he knew how inquisitive you were, he would be wise to do so. Okay. What are we both supposed to be doing, and how can we get out of it?"

There followed a stock-taking of their college commitments. Exams were in progress and there were no regular classes, but James had fixed to see two Ph.D. students that morning, and in the afternoon there was rather important departmental meeting that they ought both to attend.

"And I promised to be in my office this morning," added Paula, "for anybody who wants to come and discuss exam papers and talk about plans for next session."

She looked at James hopefully: Would he offer to deputise for her? He felt almost as strongly as she did about not disappointing a student who needed advice, and she was always willing to help him out in similar circumstances.

"You're dying to go to Whitelands, aren't you?" he said.

"So are you. And don't forget that it was you who dragged me there in the first place."

"All right. You go down there this morning and find somewhere for us to stay for the weekend, and I'll make your excuses and look after your students and go to that bloody meeting."

Paula thanked him most sincerely and resigned herself to putting up with his almost intolerable air of smugness and virtue. Why was it, she asked herself as she drove cautiously through the worst of Central London traffic, that if a woman made a little self-sacrificing gesture, it was taken for granted, but if a man did the same thing, it had to be wondered at and regarded as very praiseworthy. Would it always be thus? How would Kitty Burden answer such a question? Kitty Burden, whom it was quite impossible to categorise, who seemed to be at the same time so tough and so vulnerable, so insanely self-sacrificing for her daughter's sake and yet quite incapable of subduing her own independence of spirit. Kitty Burden, who had, with open eyes and against all expert advice, gone back into the trap that she had created for herself.

Had she intended all along to find her own way to escape? In other words, had Kitty Burden pushed her husband over the edge of the chalk-pit or perhaps got somebody else to do it for her?

The question throbbed away in Paula's mind as her eyes took pleasure in mild blue skies and a green countryside. In the corner of a field she saw a splash of scarlet. Poppies. They were a rare sight nowadays, as were so many other wild flowers. Fewer and fewer of them were being spared the chemical spray. Paula pulled the car to the side of the road and looked with joy upon the shining flowers.

But this pure little lift of the heart was short-lived. Her thoughts slipped from scarlet poppies to Henry Graverton, mathematician turned naturalist in his retirement, and to Kitty Burden's sudden interest in botany.

Searching for plants. What an excellent way to get to know the land around the village. Including the old chalk quarry. What a perfect excuse for being wherever you wanted to be. On a steep slope at the top of a chalk cliff, for instance. There might be some rare orchis there.

Paula drove on, her imagination outracing the gentle chugging of her little car. But as she came nearer to Whitelands, she found it necessary to concentrate on the driving, because suddenly there were big yellow "Diversion" signs, great white slashes in the gentle hillside, bulldozers and trucks and temporary traffic controls, and all the other paraphernalia of road-building.

So they've started, she said to herself. Whitelands is to be dragged into the real world, and Roger Aston will no longer have to open up his farm lane every time it snows.

After a long wait behind a convoy of huge vehicles from Spain, Paula at last found a sign showing how to get to Whitelands. Approaching the village in this way, through this maze of construction activity, and in midsummer, she found that it all looked completely strange to her; it seemed to have no connection at all with the snowbound community that James had brought her to only a few months ago.

Would its inhabitants seem equally strange? Would they remember her, even recognise her? And above all, whatever excuse could she make for being here?

One thing at a time, she told herself. First of all, find somewhere to stay, and then phone James. The White Horse? The Black Swan? She vaguely remembered that there was a village inn that hadn't looked particularly welcoming.

Here it was. Just The Swan, and on the sign it looked neither white nor black but a dirty yellowish grey. The house itself was modest, built of the ubiquitous flint, and near the entrance a small blackboard was propped up against the wall. On it was written in chalk in a large, clear script, "Coffee being served now."

Paula parked the mini and went in.

The saloon bar had a bare, well scrubbed wooden floor, long wooden tables and chairs, great copper bowls full of sweet peas, and shining copper utensils in the huge black fireplace. On the walls were sporting prints and a dartboard. There were no fruit machines, no juke-box, no computer games. The bar was a wooden counter at one end of which was a brass handbell and a notice in the same clear writing as that on the blackboard, saying, "Ring for Service."

Paula rang, and as she waited, she looked around with interest and satisfaction. The Swan at Whitelands was, like the red poppies, an increasing rarity in this day and age: an unmodernised Old English village inn. If there were rooms to let, and she was convinced that there were, they would be whitewashed and low-ceilinged, with high brass bedsteads and patchwork quilts lavender-scented. The plumbing would be rather unreliable, but the place would be very clean.

A vanished world. If one came across it at all, it was usually artificially re-created, but here in Whitelands it was the genuine article. Would the landlord be in keeping with his surroundings? Paula rather hoped not: that would be almost too perfect. She was quite relieved to see a short, dark girl with a mildly punk hair-style appear from behind the bar.

"I'd like some coffee, please," she said. "And is it possible to have a double room for a night or two?"

"I'll have to ask my father, but I think it will be okay."

The voice and the manner were rather aloof and did not invite conversation. Paula took her coffee and sat down at one of the scrubbed wooden tables. This would be for James to handle, she decided. He was much better than she was at getting information out of strangers. She followed the punk girl up a narrow staircase into a room that was very much like that of her imagination, and asked if she might use a telephone and whether they served an evening meal.

Ten minutes later she was standing by he counter in the saloon bar, telling James all about it. The punk girl had disappeared, and there was nobody else in sight.

"So what are you going to do now?" asked James.

"I'd like to plunge right in and go to Boyds, but I don't know what sort of reception I'd get. Both Roger and Kitty are equally crazy in their different ways, and I've got a feeling that Philip wouldn't be pleased to see me."

"You've been very kind to Kitty," James reminded her. "You've got a right to ask how she is, if nothing else."

"I suppose so, but they don't go by the usual social conventions. Not in Whitelands. I think maybe I'd better go and call at the vicarage. At least they'll behave in a civilised way. And they'll know that I've come mostly out of sheer inquisitiveness, so there will be no need for any pretending."

"Good luck. Eight o'clock at The Swan then. I hope they produce a good dinner. There's a long line of students to see you, and I'm not going to get much time for lunch."

"You want me to thank you again. I do thank you, you know, and I also wish you were here now."

"Go and talk to the vicar. I'm sure he's a prime suspect. Good-bye."

Paula walked slowly up the village street. The cottage gardens were full of colour, the porches festooned with climbing roses. The great mound of the churchyard, with its yew trees, which in winter had seemed sombre and even menacing, now provided a pleasing contrast to the bright gardens.

To her left was The Twitten, Bill Burden's house. It looked larger than Paula remembered it. Perhaps the snow had had a diminishing effect. It also looked slightly less well cared for than some of the other dwellings in the village, slightly less perfect. "Neglected" would be too strong a word, but Paula noticed that the edges of the lawns were somewhat ragged and there were weeds under the standard rose-trees. The gate had been left open, but that could have been done by the postman or some other caller.

She looked to her left. The gate at the end of the private road that led to Boyds was also open, wide open and propped back against the fence. The track itself was rough and chalky. On either side were fields of shining corn. He lets out the land, Paula reminded herself, and wondered what sort of bold person would dare to become a tenant of Roger Aston. Was there some neighbouring farmer who was hoping to take over the lot? More likely that a property development company was after it. It was a most suitable position for a high-class housing estate.

Paula smiled to herself. That would solve Roger's financial difficulties, but if he could not even endure the sympathetic assistance of one of the big national preservation societies, then how on earth would he behave towards the people who wanted to build on his land?

But perhaps, she thought as she turned away, Roger's own scheme would succeed in spite of all the obstacles to it. At any rate, the first of these was now out of the way: Bill Burden was dead, and Kitty was under Roger's roof. In fact, it could well be the old Viking himself who had engineered Bill's fall. He was as though and active as any of the younger suspects.

I must find out what people are saying, Paula told herself as she walked through the lych-gate into the churchyard.

The vicarage, somewhat to her surprise, was a comparatively new building, probably dating from the 1930s. A rather dingy-looking gabled house, overshadowed by a couple of fine beech trees. The engine of a lawn-mower started up as Paula approached the gate, and a moment later Mr. Fulham himself appeared round the corner of the house. He was looking down at the mower and did not see her. Paula watched him proceed along the full length of the lawn. Like everything else in the village, he looked different in summer dress: taller than she remembered, perhaps rather younger, and his handling of the mower showed impatience and irritation rather than a careful attention to the task.

Paula was wondering whether he would be glad or sorry to be

interrupted, when he glanced up and saw her standing at the gate. He switched off the motor and looked at her for a moment without recognition. Then he said, "Forgive me, but I'm rather bad at remembering names."

"Paula Glenning. We met one snowy day last January, when Mrs. Burden was taken to hospital suffering from an overdose of drugs."

"Yes, of course. You were one of the London visitors who got caught up in the drama. No doubt you have heard the latest development?"

"Professor Burden's death? Yes, that's why I'm here."

"To comfort the widow?"

This was said with a lift of the eyebrows, which instantly recalled to Paula the somewhat prickly, sardonic character that she remembered.

"I'd like to try to do that, among other things," she said, "but I thought I'd better know, first of all, what happened. The radio news item didn't say much."

"And I can't tell much, but you're welcome to what I know. Shall we sit in the shade?"

He led the way to a couple of garden chairs placed under one of the beech trees.

"Is Mr. Goff with you?" he asked as they sat down.

"He's coming this evening. We're staying at The Swan."

"You couldn't do better. It's a place for connoisseurs."

Paula felt complimented and rather more at ease.

"What are the people like who run it?" she asked.

"Father and daughter. Ken Hodges and Pat. Mother ran away. Taciturn but efficient. It's not the village gossip-shop, you know. For that you'll have to go a couple of miles along the main road to the Sussex Inn."

"Thank you," said Paula, feeling less comfortable again and telling herself that Mr. Robert Fulham was not what one expected in a parish priest. In fact, he rather reminded her of some of her academic colleagues, whose edgy manners and uncertain tempers were no help at all in the peaceful running of their department. James was probably putting up with some of them at this very moment, trying to smooth over the prickles.

It helped to think of James.

"Mr. Fulham," she said more confidently, "you will think, and everybody will think, that I've come here out of sheer meddling inquisitiveness, like the people who rush to look at a disaster. I am very inquisitive, but I never run to disasters, and I wouldn't be here if I hadn't felt very concerned indeed—humanly concerned—about Kitty Burden. She came to stay with me in London after she recovered from that overdose last January, and we got quite close. I thought it was most unwise of her to come back to her husband, but she was determined to do so, and I haven't heard from her since. I feel that she needs—and I don't care how crazy this sounds—I feel she needs saving, and I had an idea I might be able to do something about it."

Paula stopped rather breathlessly. She had not intended to speak like this at all, but having spoken, she found that she had clarified her own attitude and spoken the truth as far as she knew it. There was something about Robert Fulham's manner that made pretence very difficult but at the same time made you feel the need to explain yourself. Perhaps, after all, in spite of the lack of easy sympathy, he was not such a bad guardian of the human conscience and spirit.

"You may be able to help her," he said, and his voice now sounded troubled and not at all critical. "She certainly needs help."

"You've seen her?"

"Yes. I've only just got back from Boyds. She wanted to come home, and the Astons, father and son, didn't want her to. She appealed to me, and I more or less abducted her. I believe she will be pleased to see you, and we will walk over together presently. I doubt if she will open the door to you if I don't come too."

"Oh, poor Kitty!"

Paula's exclamation was spontaneous and heartfelt.

"Yes indeed," said the vicar. "At least the police and the newshounds seem to have departed for the time being, but there are plenty of other interested parties around. She would really do best to go right away until the inquest."

"Do you think she would come away with me?"

"You must ask her."

"Mr. Fulham—"

"The name is Robert. Not Bob, please."

"Robert. What has *really* been happening to the Burdens these last months, and what really happened last night?"

The vicar laughed, and Paula thought suddenly, Why, he's by no means unattractive and he isn't all that old. It is the elderliness of his sister that has somehow brushed off onto him. Had he ever had a wife? Could it possibly be that Kitty—

Hastily she shut down the lid upon the suspicions that were beginning to emerge. Speculation could come later; now was the moment for facts and for retaining the good relationship that she had at last succeeded in establishing between herself and the Reverend Robert Fulham.

"Sorry," she said, "that's a silly way to put it. When we were here before and talking about Bill and Kitty Burden, I remember your saying that their troubles were upsetting the whole village community and that you wished they would move into Brighton and leave Whitelands in peace."

"Did I say that? How very tactless of me. I certainly felt it at the time, but I have to admit that the situation seemed to improve after that traumatic weekend. At any rate, they kept their differences much more to themselves."

"When James saw Bill in London," said Paula tentatively, "he said that Kitty had taken up botanising and good works."

Robert Fulham laughed again. "Very true. She has been making quite strenuous efforts to join in the life of the community. My sister has been very glad of her help with the Women's Aid Group. They raise funds for Third World charities."

"And the botanising?"

"Ah, that was Henry Graverton. He and Louise were so shocked by the events of that weekend that they determined to break their rule of never meddling in other people's affairs. Kitty has always been interested in wildlife, and Bill appeared quite satisfied to let her go exploring with the happy couple, since it made *her* happy and consequently more indulgent to-wards himself."

"So they had achieved some sort of balance," commented Paula, forbearing to remark that, as far as she could recall, Lou-ise Graverton had not been in the habit of accompanying her husband on his botanising excursions.

"It certainly looked as if they had," said the vicar. "You sound disappointed."

"Not disappointed. Just rather surprised. What has Bill been doing while Kitty was integrating herself into the community?"

"Writing a little. Giving his expert opinion on various chat shows. He's been in London quite a lot, as no doubt you already know."

"So you don't think he slipped down the cliff on purpose?"

"I can't possibly answer that question," replied the vicar. "All I can say is that he has shown no more signs of discontent with his marriage and that the accusation that his wife was trying to poison him has never been repeated. He does not confide in me. Philip Aston might be able to tell you more about his state of mind, although it seems to me that that friendship has been dwindling in recent months."

"What about your sister? Did he talk to her?"

Robert did not immediately answer, and Paula had the impres-sion that the question disturbed him.

"Yes," he said at last. "My sister is a very sympathetic listener. Unlike myself. She does not pass on to me other people's confi-dences, but she has told the police that in her opinion Professor Burden was in a calm and contented state of mind yesterday, with no particular worries. I won't say any more. Perhaps you will have the opportunity of talking to her yourself. She's taken the car and gone into Brighton to do some shopping, but she'll be back this afternoon."

"Thank you," said Paula, and for a moment or two they remained silent, staring at the expanse of rather overgrown lawn and the privet hedge beyond.

He's not going to tell me any more, thought Paula, but I can't complain: he's given a very clear impression of how things have been on the surface. Does he really want me to go away? Does he think that I might be of some help to Kitty?

It was impossible to tell. "I'm taking up a lot of your time," she said aloud. "If you could spare me a few more minutes to come over to The Twitten with me—"

"Certainly."

As they walked through the churchyard, Paula said, "So the Preservation Society lost the battle over the new road-works, I see."

"It was bound to, and over the oil, though fortunately they didn't find any worth drilling for. In fact, the society itself has become somewhat moribund since Bill Burden lost interest in it. Roger Aston is too eccentric and unreliable to lead any effective campaign."

"Yes indeed." Paula smiled. "He'll draw his sword and raise the flag, but he'll never cope with officialdom."

They reached the front door of the Burdens' house. The vicar pressed the bell three times—long, short, long.

"We'll have to wait a minute or two," he said. "She will know my ring, but she'll probably make sure by looking out of a window. Stand back where she can see you."

Paula did so. A window on the first floor was opened and shut again immediately. There was a short anxious interval before the front door was opened.

"I'll leave you," said Robert. "I'll be at home if you want me."

11

"So you've come."

That was all Kitty said for the first couple of minutes.

She locked and bolted the front door and led the way into the sitting-room. The curtains were drawn across the window in front of the house, but the window at the side, with the view over fields, was open and uncurtained, and the black-and-white cat was perched on the window-sill in the sunshine.

Kitty took Paula by the hand, drew her towards the settee, sat down, pulled Paula down beside her, and clutched her hand as if she could never let it go.

Paula waited in silence. Kitty looked stylish in a pale blue linen dress. Her dark hair was sleek and shining, her make-up carefully applied. Apart from the fact that she was thinner than ever, there was no hint of the shabby, aging woman that she had appeared to be while she was staying at Paula's flat.

Nor was there any sign of hysteria, of lack of control. Only that frantic, steely grip under which Paula's own fingers were beginning to turn numb revealed the tension within her.

At last she relaxed and said, perfectly calmly, "I'm so glad to see you. Would you like some coffee?"

"Thank you, but I had some at the pub. The Swan. I've booked a room there. James is joining me this evening."

"You wouldn't rather stay here? No, perhaps not," she added immediately. "You must have horrible memories of this house, both of you. And I can't cope with being hostess all the time. No, it's better that you're down in the village. You must use the same code as Robert when you come to the door. A long ring, a short one, a long one. Don't try to phone. I'm not answering. And I'm not going out. Would you like some coffee? No. I've already asked that. Shall I make us some lunch?"

"That would be nice," said Paula, recognising the eagerness with which the question was asked. "Would you like me to come into the kitchen to help? Or shall I wait here?"

"You'd better wait, I think. I have to adjust my thoughts. I'm still rather confused. I didn't really want to go to Boyds last night, but Phil insisted. And he got Dr. Shore along, and she gave me a knock-out shot of something. And this morning it was all police and newspapers. Philip was wonderful, I must say. But, oh, Paula!" For the first time her voice shook. "I don't want to marry him. I don't want to exchange one trap for another. It'll be just the same. Except that he's not quite such a shit as Bill was."

"He wants to marry you?"

"Lord, yes. We could have a relationship. Not too bad, provided I didn't make a fuss about his men friends, and he wouldn't make a fuss about mine. But I'm sick of it. I want . . . I want to live with a man I love. Or else with nobody."

"But Kitty."

Paula followed her into the kitchen. It seemed, after all, that Kitty did not need to be alone to adjust her ideas. "Kitty, you don't have to marry anybody. You're free. Bill's dead and you're free."

"Yes. I'm free." Kitty stood still with a knife and fork in her hand. "I'm free," she repeated in a puzzled voice, as if she did not know the meaning of the word.

"You don't want to decide upon anything at all. Not yet. If you want to get away for a while, come and stay with me."

"Thank you," said Kitty in the same dazed manner. Then suddenly she became brisk. "We'll use these mugs." She reached up to a cupboard. "We can be as sloppy as we like. We don't have to put on an act for anybody. Help yourself from the fridge. There's salad and cold meat. I'm going to have a tray on my lap. Don't answer that phone. Let it ring."

They carried their lunch into the sitting-room, and the black-and-white cat leapt down from the window-sill and came over to sniff at Kitty's plate.

"Here you are, Merry," she said, throwing it a piece of chicken and patting the cushion beside her. "You can come and sit here. Come on." She hugged the cat. "No more rules now. You can scratch the chairs as much as you like. We're free." She put her face down against the silky little head. "We're free now, Merry. Free, free, free!"

She let go of the cat, which settled down neatly on the cushion, paws tucked in, head on one side, looking at Kitty in what Paula felt sure was a rather bewildered manner.

"I'm sorry," said Kitty to Paula. "I can't really believe it, you know. I feel this is all a dream."

"Yes," Paula said, but made no further comment. She had a suspicion that there was now a bit of acting mixed up with Kitty's genuine shock and distress. This had not been so when she first arrived. The welcome had been completely spontaneous, and so had Kitty's remarks about Philip, but during the last few minutes she had been recovering enough to become calculating: how could she keep Paula's sympathy, how could she keep Paula on her side?

The sympathy was certainly there, but it was mingled with wariness. Every time she had come into close contact with Kitty, thought Paula as she ate the chicken salad, she had felt the same: irritation and compassion mixed in almost equal measures. How could one ever be quite sure that Kitty was telling the truth? Perhaps shock tactics might help.

"Kitty," she said abruptly, pushing aside her plate, "did you push Bill over that cliff?"

"Would you expect me to tell you if I had?"

She sounded alert, watchful, not in the least vague or confused.

"Yes, I would," said Paula bluntly.

"Why would you expect me to tell you? Why should I trust you with a confession of murder?"

"Because you do trust me. Because when you opened the door to me, you were enormously relieved to see somebody to whom you knew you could tell the truth."

"Yes. I did feel like that. I felt that you were somebody who would not use any confession, any truth, against me."

"Thank you. That is a great compliment."

"Cigarette?" asked Kitty.

Paula nodded, and they smoked in silence for a minute or two. The telephone rang again, but neither of them took any notice.

"I didn't kill my husband," said Kitty presently, "but I am in great difficulties over his death. Supposing I had convinced you that I had killed him; then purely as a matter of academic interest, what would you do?"

"Get up, say goodbye, and go right out of your life for ever after. I think that's what I should do."

Kitty laughed, and Paula caught a glimpse of a different character, open, lively, and good company.

"I believe you are capable of doing just that," she said. "But I don't think you would be able to keep it quite to yourself. I think you would tell James."

"Would I?"

"Yes, Paula, you would. That's the difference between you and me. If something needs to be kept secret, I can keep it secret. For ever, if need be, whatever the provocation, whatever the cost. Could you do that? No, I don't think you could. Not quite."

"Perhaps you're right. Or perhaps I haven't yet been tried."

Again they smoked in silence.

"So you didn't push Bill," said Paula at last. "But you know who did."

Kitty made no reply. The telephone rang again.

"Shall I unplug it?" suggested Paula.

"No. I feel I can stand it now, and it might be the police."
Kitty crushed out her cigarette and lifted the receiver.

"Sergeant Adams? Yes, it's Mrs. Burden. I'm back home. No,
you didn't disturb me. I have a friend from London here. She
will stay for a while . . . The inquest will be next Thursday?
That's quick, isn't it? . . . Thank you very much for letting me
know . . . No, I'm afraid I haven't yet gone through the papers
on my husband's desk. I'll do so as soon as I can, and if I find
anything that might be helpful, I'll let you know."

She replaced the phone. "A nice young man. Very anxious not
to distress the widow."

"So nobody is suspecting you."

"I wouldn't say that. I'd only say that the police seem to think
it was an accident. Do you want to go and survey the scene?"

Gentle mockery was now in her voice.

"Purely as a matter of academic interest," replied Paula in
similar tones, "yes, I would like to see the spot."

"Then let's go."

"I thought you were hiding yourself away. Coded bell-rings
and all that sort of thing."

"That was when I felt so alone. But I feel quite different with
you here. What sort of shoes have you got on? Yes, those will
do. It's quite rough walking in places."

They set out along the path between the house and the
churchyard. Very soon it turned into a steep and narrow track,
bordered by thick gorse bushes. They climbed steadily, saying
very little. Where the path widened into a grassy track they
stopped and looked back at the village nestling among the beech
trees at the foot of the slope.

"It's a lovely spot," said Paula. "A pity it's been such an unhappy home for you."

"My own fault entirely." Kitty was brusque. "But these last
few months I really have been doing my best."

"I believe you. Shall we go on?"

They walked on in silence, side by side, until the path narrowed again.

"There's the bottom of the chalk-pit," said Kitty. "Between those bushes on your left. You can just see it. Careful. These bushes are very prickly. We can get through over here. This must be where they brought him out."

Paula followed Kitty through the gap. The whole area was very much overgrown. Even on the white cliff itself there were tufts of grass and little clumps of wild flowers.

"Isn't it extraordinary," remarked Paula, "how things can grow without any soil and even without much moisture."

"Yes, isn't it? They fascinate me, these chalk flowers, that live on so little," said Kitty. "Look, here's a round-headed rampion. Lovely rich blue."

"And lots of harebells," said Paula, doing a bit of exploring on her own. "And these little yellow vetchlike things. I've forgotten the name. What a pity that one forgets so much of what one learned as a child."

"I know, but one soon picks it up again. I wonder where he fell." Kitty was pushing her way to the foot of the cliff. "It must be somewhere about here. Look—some of the cliff came down with him. And the bushes are all crushed. Oh, Paula."

"Do you want to go home?"

"No. Let's go on. It's better to see for myself rather than to keep on imagining." Kitty looked up the side of the cliff, shading her eyes against the sun. "What a height it is. But people have survived greater falls. Supposing he hadn't been killed. Supposing he'd been seriously crippled. Oh no." She began to laugh. "Not two of them. A disabled husband a disabled daughter."

The laughter seemed in danger of going out of control.

"Don't think of it," said Paula sharply. "It didn't happen. What did they actually say was the cause of death?"

"Oh, the usual. Multiple injuries. I didn't have to see him. There was plenty of others to do the identifying. Louise, in particular. Poor old Louise. She was flashing her torch around at the foot of the cliff while the others were hunting some distance away, and she saw him all tangled up in the gorse bushes. All those thorns. That's enough to draw blood. She must have had a dreadful shock. Unless she already knew. But why should Louise Graverton want to get rid of Bill?"

Kitty was talking very quickly and excitedly, as if only just holding on to her self-control. There was no doubt that she was very agitated, as indeed she had reason to be, but Paula once more had the impression that she was aiming to create an effect.

"You'd think the last thing Louise wanted was to get rid of Bill and leave me free to annex her precious Henry," went on Kitty.

"Is that your intention?"

Paula decided that the best way to cope with these moods of Kitty's was to be very matter-of-fact.

"My intention? To annex Henry? Do you really believe that?"

"I've no opinion on the matter at all. You raised the subject, so I'm asking you the question."

Kitty blinked. Perhaps it was the brightness of the sun; or perhaps she was a bit surprised at Paula's reaction needed to bring her thoughts into focus.

"I'm talking stupidly," she said at last. "As you have realised, and you are not going to let me go on with it. You always see through me. That's why it's such a relief to be with you. But it's also very difficult. When your whole life is a pretence and suddenly there is no need to pretend, then who are you? What are you? Suppose you genuinely do not know?"

"I can understand that very well," said Paula, "but you still haven't answered my question."

"I can't remember what it was. Oh, yes. Henry Graverton. He's a sweetie. Much more interesting and much more alive than he appears to be when he's in company with his wife. He's helped me a lot over these last few months, and I'm very grateful. But he's not the love of my life and he knows it. You want to know whether I've given him any cause to believe that if he got rid of Bill for me— That's it, isn't it, Paula?"

"You've said it. I didn't. But yes, it did enter my mind."

"Henry as murderer? No, I don't buy it. I don't say that he isn't attracted to me, because that wouldn't be true, but he's certainly not going to put his partnership with Louise at risk. They suit each other. They are a genuinely contented couple. You don't often find one. Shall we go on up to the top of the cliff?"

Kitty was walking back to the path as she spoke, and after a last quick glance around, Paula followed her. She would have liked to spend some time alone at this spot, pondering in peace about the personalities involved, sorting out her own impressions. Although Kitty had seemed to switch back into sincerity, Paula still had the feeling that she was being led by her, mentally as well as physically, and only when she was alone would she be able to stand back and make her own judgments.

The path now turned quite sharply to the right and became much steeper.

"All right?" asked Kitty, stopping to look at Paula.

It was, indeed, quite a climb, a sort of natural staircase composed of clumps of rough grass in the surrounding chalk. To the left was a fence made of wooden posts linked by wire. It didn't look very substantial, and it gave little to hold on to. Nevertheless, for an active person, even an elderly active person like Bill Burden, there should be no great difficulty, provided one took reasonable care. If it were wet though, the path could be slippery and even rather dangerous.

But last night it had not been wet: there had been no rain for many days.

They came out at last upon a gentle slope of short downland turf, springy to the feet, as soft to walk on as a carpet.

"Oh," said Paula, somewhat disappointed. "I thought we would be able to see the sea."

"Not yet. There's quite a way further to go. But look around, look inland."

Paula did so and exclaimed in delight at the land spread out below: clusters of roofs, with here and there a church tower, clumps of trees, little fields, the distant shimmer of the water of a reservoir, the blue heat haze of the horizon.

"It's even better along here," said Kitty, turning left alongside the fence. "This is the place the ramblers mostly come to."

A couple moved off as they approached, elderly walkers, the woman wearing tweeds and solid shoes, the man in brown corduroy trousers and a jacket patched with leather at the elbows.

"At least there aren't any sightseers," said Kitty. "But then Bill never did anything to make him notorious."

"Professors of economics are hardly pop stars," agreed Paula. "One forgets what a small world we academics live in."

They walked on for a few yards, and then Kitty exclaimed, "Look out! You're going too near."

Paula had not noticed. The fence, which was in any case a flimsy protection, was now entwined with bushes. She stopped and saw that these bushes were in fact growing on the very edge of the cliff. To grasp at them if one slipped would very likely bring the whole lot down. It looked as if this was what Bill might have done. If she, walking in broad daylight, could be so careless, surely somebody walking by the light of the moon and the stars would be at much greater risk.

Hastily she removed herself to a safer place before surveying the area. This little episode had been very revealing indeed and worth any amount of talk and speculation. She had seen and felt for herself how very easy it was to meet with an accident here, and she did not think that the warning notice, which was partially obscured by brambles, was anything like an adequate protection. Somebody would have to put up a much more solid fence, and do it soon, if further tragedies were to be avoided.

Paula found herself growing quite indignant, but at the same time she was conscious of a sense of relief. No wonder Dr. Shore had been so definite on the telephone when she said that the verdict of the coroner would be accidental death. Suicide seemed unlikely in the extreme. But unless some very conclusive evidence were to come to light, it would be quite impossible to prove that anybody other than Bill himself had been involved.

There was not going to be any official murder hunt.

But the moment Paula had convinced herself of this, she found that she was becoming dissatisfied again. Bill's death was too convenient. Either Kitty had pushed him, or somebody else had done it for her. Roger, Philip, Henry Graverton, and the vicar. These were the four that seemed most likely, with Glenys Fulham and Louise Graverton as possible suspects whose motives Paula could not yet begin to guess at.

Somebody had taken advantage of the lie of the land and the neglect of the local authority. It must be so. People so heartily disliked as Bill Burden had been simply did not have accidents like this one.

Paula looked around for Kitty. She was now some distance away, half-hidden by a blackberry bush, bending down as if she had noticed something. Was she searching for evidence? Or planting some evidence? Surely the police had gone over the ground thoroughly.

"Found anything?" called out Paula.

"It's only coltsfoot," Kitty shouted back and came nearer before she spoke again. "I thought it might be something interesting."

So she was still thinking about wild plants, or at any rate she was pretending to.

"Where exactly did Bill fall?" asked Paula.

"I don't know. I was wondering that myself."

"Well, it can't be where you were standing just now, because the fence isn't broken there. It must be somewhere near the place where I nearly went over the edge myself."

Moving with care, they went over the ground together.

"You could have pushed me over just now," said Paula, "and nobody would ever have known that I hadn't slipped."

"If you had survived and remembered what I had done, then they would have known."

"Not necessarily. You could have done it in such a way that even I myself would have thought you were trying to save me."

"I suppose so." Kitty did not sound very interested.

"Did you push Bill?"

I'm crazy, thought Paula as she asked this question. I'm giving her the best possible motive and the best possible opportunity to do the same to me. Of course, she didn't believe me when I said that if she confessed, I would just go away and keep quiet about it for ever after. Of course, she feels me to be a threat. But, paradoxically, she needs me, just because she feels that I've come closer to her than anybody else has. Closer even than the man she loves. If there is indeed such a man.

Kitty did not reply, and they stood there on the soft turf, close together but without speaking, for what seemed to Paula a long time. In front was the chequered landscape, behind them the grassy slope. A couple of riders came by, teenage girls on big chestnut horses. Paula and Kitty turned their heads and watched them canter over the brow of the hill.

"Were you up here last night?" asked Paula when they were once more alone.

"You're not going to believe me when I say I wasn't," replied Kitty in a voice that sounded full of sadness.

"If only I could be sure. I want to be sure that it was an accident. How can I ever be sure?"

"There's no way. You're never going to be sure that I'm not a murderer. You find it very difficult to live with uncertainty, don't you, Paula?"

"Yes. I'm sorry, but I do."

"Don't apologise. It doesn't worry me at all. You are the one who suffers from it. Shall we go back?"

Paula followed her down the path back to the village, thinking more about herself now than about Kitty. Difficult to live with uncertainty. How very true that was. Kitty was by no means the first person to say this to her, but it had never struck her with such force as at this moment.

Was it a weakness of character? Perhaps it was. At any rate, it was not a weakness that extended to her teaching, to her scholarship. In the study and appreciation of great works of literature there could be no certainties: each new reader must discover the works afresh and make his or her own individual contact with the mind of the creator. It was in her daily life among her fellow human beings, thought Paula, that she always needed to know, to be quite sure.

An enquiring mind? Or a search for certainties? Was there any difference between the two?

She decided to ask James about it when he arrived at Whitelands this evening, and then almost immediately afterwards she decided not to. This was something that she was going to think about and worry out for herself until she reached some sort of resolution.

There she went again, chasing after an answer. It was no good. She was not going to be able to leave it alone. Very probably she would never know. If whoever it was kept their nerve and kept quiet, then nobody would ever know. The only thing that Paula could be absolutely certain of was that she herself was never going to be able to stop wondering.

12

When they came to the bottom end of the path, Kitty peered over the wall of her garden, hastily drew back again, and whispered to Paula, "Roger's there. Lying in wait. I can't stand it. I'm going to hide at the vicarage."

She hurried towards the lych-gate. Paula ran to keep up with her.

"When are you coming back?"

"When it's safe. Why don't you ask Roger what he was doing yesterday evening?"

"What d'you mean, Kitty?"

"He came past the house and up this path at about half past nine. I was up in my room, and I looked out of the window and saw him. I haven't told anybody else but you. Goodbye. See you later."

Kitty pulled away, leaving Paula yet again with the sensation of being manipulated to serve Kitty's own purposes. For a moment she was filled with frustration and resentment, as well as an anger that was partly directed towards herself. She had a strong impulse to go back to The Swan straight away, collect her car, and amuse herself as best she could until James arrived.

Why did she have to torment herself with insoluble problems on this bright summer day in this pleasant countryside? Sensible people were out riding or walking or attending to their gardens or driving down to the coast to swim or sail.

Paula walked out of the end of The Twitten and across the road towards the village street. She told herself that she would not have stopped to look back at Kitty's house, had it not been for Roger Aston's mighty shout.

He was at the gate and was coming after her; it was impossible to escape.

"Didn't I see you with Kitty? Don't I know you?"

The white hair looked even more wild than she remembered, the face redder than ever.

"We met last winter," she said politely, "when the village was snowed up. You let us use your road and invited us in to coffee."

"That's it. I knew I knew you. Never forget a face. Nor a name. Funny name. Like a boy's. Bit foreign-sounding. Don't tell me. I'll get it. Petra. That's it. Petra."

Paula found it quite impossible to contradict him. He seemed to take it for granted that she was going to accompany him as he set off with large strides along Boyds Lane.

Why not, she thought, struggling to keep up; perhaps I might learn something new. At any rate it could hardly be worse than being with Kitty. In fact, Roger was so very self-centered that it was almost restful to be with him. Provided one made the right sort of noises now and then, he was content. This was a relief from the disagreeable sensation of being watched and manipulated.

"How difficult it all looks in summer," she said when the pace had slowed down and she could get her breath.

The answer was a grunt.

"I see they have started on the road-works."

Another grunt. Paula had expected a strong reaction, either of approval or disapproval. She could not guess which it would be, for Roger was entirely unpredictable.

"Is Philip with you?" she asked as they approached the house.

"Coming back this evening," he replied. "Had to go to London. Got a job, y'know. Can't neglect his work. Not even for Kitty."

He hurried on again. Paula dragged behind, admiring the proportions of the old house, its appeal now enhanced by the background of trees in leaf and green fields. A fat white duck came out of the pond as she strolled by, and waddled towards her.

"But I've nothing for you," she said aloud, momentarily transported back to childhood and to the joy of feeding ducks.

Roger, who had reached the far side of the pond, stopped and turned round. "Hurry up, Petra!" he roared. "I'm going to make you some coffee. You liked our coffee."

"Yes, I did," she called back, but doubted whether he heard her.

The hall looked shabbier than ever, and even on this summer day one could feel the chill. How did Kitty behave when she was at Boyds, wondered Paula. She could not give herself an answer. Kitty was many-faceted, chameleonlike. Paula had seen for herself the "sophisticated hostess" act, the "sardonic mocking" act, the "desperate self-hurting victim" act, and had caught a brief glimpse, behind all these and no doubt many other acts, of a lovely, humorous, intelligent personality.

"In the breakfast-room," said Roger, and Paula followed him along the passage. As far as she could judge, this room looked just the same, warm now from the sunshine and in its odd way quite welcoming.

"Sit down," said Roger. "I'll make you coffee."

Paula obeyed, taking a chair by the table from which she could look at the portrait of Philip's mother. What had her life been like, this dark Mediterranean beauty in the light blue uniform? Had she felt herself trapped? Or had she loved Roger so much that it did not feel that way? It would not be so very difficult to love Roger, for all his faults; to love him protectively, sheltering his essential innocence, his vulnerability behind all the bluster. One would love him as his son, Philip, loved him—with irritable devotion.

Kitty was capable of this sort of love, thought Paula suddenly; and equally suddenly she felt that Kitty would be perfectly capable of adapting herself to life at Boyds if she wanted to. It would be full of daily annoyances and frustrations, but it would not have the deep emotional insecurity and unhappiness of life with Bill.

Kitty could do it; but Kitty was not going to do it, not so much because she wanted to be free, as because she loved another man. More and more Paula was becoming convinced that that man was Robert Fulham, vicar of St. Anne's Church at Whitelands.

The sound of heavy footsteps warned of Roger's return. He came in carrying a tray, set it down on the table, and poured out the coffee with an air of great self-satisfaction. Then he watched anxiously while Paula took up her cup.

It was weak, tasteless stuff, but Paula drank it with every appearance of appreciation, remembering Philip's remark that his father never put enough coffee in.

"Lovely," she said. "Thank you."

If one lived here, she thought, one would have to develop all sorts of little subterfuges in order to keep warm, get enough to eat, and keep clean; but it might not be so very difficult. Roger would probably be quite manageable once his trust and affection were gained.

"I'll tell Philip," said Roger. "He never thinks I can do anything right at all."

"How is Philip?"

"Worried. Very worried." Roger sat down heavily. "You know Bill Burden is dead?"

"Yes indeed."

"Fell into the chalk-pit. Silly ass. Should have known it's dangerous to go too near the edge. These clever people. Professor! Ha!"

Roger emitted a sound that was part-shout, part-laugh. It was very loud and sudden, and was accompanied by a thump on the table. Paula, startled into nearly dropping her cup, decided that although Roger might be manageable, to live at close quarters with him would be rather a strain on the nerves.

"Serves him right," he went on rather more quietly. "And good riddance for Kitty. But we're worried about Kitty, Petra. Shock, of course. That's only natural. But surely she couldn't really have cared for the fellow?"

Roger leaned forward confidentially, resting one large hand on the table. Paula had a vivid impression of very white hair, very red face, very blue eyes, astonishingly blue for a man of his age. Those eyes were disconcerting because they did not seem to see what others saw. Their owner lived in a world of his own.

"I'm quite sure that Kitty never cared for Bill," said Paula carefully.

She spoke what she believed, but indeed she would not have dared to say anything else. Roger's looks, Roger's behaviour during the last few minutes was causing her to revise her opinion of him as a comparatively harmless eccentric old man. He was more than eccentric; on the subject of Bill and Kitty Burden he was obsessed.

Supposing it was Roger who had pushed Bill Burden over the cliff; would he be mad enough to admit it, even boast of it? Or would he have enough sense of self-preservation to keep quiet? Ask him what he was doing on the hill path last evening, Kitty had said. Ask him yourself, thought Paula. I'm certainly not going to do so, not when I'm alone with him.

Aloud she said, "I think that the marriage was a purely business arrangement."

"That's right. A business arrangement. What a clever girl you are, Petra, to see that. Of course it was business. Bill paid for the child; Kitty looked after the house. Made a good job of it, too. Eh? Eh?"

He looked more normal now. The intensely blue stare that saw only his own dreams had somewhat dimmed, but Paula still felt alarmed.

"I'd better go now," she said, standing up. "Kitty will be wondering where I am."

"That's right. You go and look after Kitty. Poor little Kitty.

Shock, of course. It must be shock. Needs another woman at a time like this. Much better for her to have another woman, not that priest fellow. Who does he think he is, barging in like that? We don't go to church, Phil and I. Never have done. Neither did Kitty till they got hold of her, the two of them. Meddling do-gooders.''

Roger had got up and was standing by the door of the breakfast-room talking more to himself than to Paula. She made no attempt to interrupt him. From his ramblings, she might discover something of interest.

"There was a time," said Roger in a sad, nostalgic voice, "when a parson and his wife knew their place. Sermons on Sunday. Help for the poor. Never used to interfere in other people's affairs like— Are you going, Petra?"

"Yes, I had better go now," said Paula.

I'm sure he doesn't even realise that Glenys is Robert Fulham's sister, she was saying to herself; I'm sure he thinks that Glenys is the vicar's wife. It's just the sort of mistake that an old man so totally absorbed in his own schemes might make; and if that's the case, then no doubt Kitty has been encouraging him in his mistake.

"You go and talk to Kitty," said Roger, taking her arm and almost dragging her along the corridor. "Get her away from that little slyboots Mrs. the Vicar. Don't trust the woman at all. Not at all."

They reached the front door, but he still held her arm.

"You tell Kitty, you tell Kitty—"

"Yes, I'll tell Kitty," said Paula as soothingly as she could.

"It mustn't go wrong now."

Roger sounded as if he was about to burst into tears. All the bluster had gone: he was a lonely, pathetic old man.

"It can't go wrong now, not now he's out of the way. If Kitty won't play and if it's all been for nothing—"

"I'm sure it won't go wrong," murmured Paula, after waiting in vain for him to complete the sentence.

When after a few more attempted reassurances she escaped at last, she asked herself, Does he realise that his remarks could easily be taken as an admission of guilt? What a pity that she had not been able to find out anything about his movements last night. Perhaps she could try again, with James as protection.

Deep in thought, she walked back along Boyds Lane towards the village and was approaching Kitty's house when she heard somebody speak to her.

"Excuse me." It was a woman's voice. "Haven't we met before? Weren't you there that dreadful night when Mrs. Burden took an overdose of drugs?"

Paula looked up and saw a plump middle-aged woman wearing a long, loose floral-printed dress. She was shutting the gate of The Twitten and coming towards her.

"You don't remember me. Elizabeth Reid. The Whitelands Pottery."

"Oh, yes. I'm sorry. My mind was miles away."

"Dr. Glenning, isn't it? I saw Miss Fulham in the butcher's just now, and said you were here."

"I thought the vicar said that his sister had gone to Brighton," said Paula, trying to recover from the shock of discovering how quickly news flows round a village.

"She had, but she came back to get the meat. She always likes to support the local tradespeople as much as possible."

This had to be counted as a remark of approval, since presumably Mrs. Reid was among the local tradespeople.

"Have you been to see Mrs. Burden?" asked Paula.

"Yes, but she's not there. Or she's not answering."

"Oh. That's a pity. I was rather hoping to see her. Perhaps she's at the vicarage. I'm staying at The Swan," she added as they began to walk down the village street together. "Just for a couple of nights. I expect Miss Glenys Fulham told you that as well."

Paula was not quite sure how this remark would be received, and was glad to hear her companion laugh.

"Yes, she did. That's rural life for you. A visitor from London is a newsworthy event."

"My experience of Whitelands," said Paula, also smiling, "has been very far from uneventful. Kitty Burden takes an overdose and is rushed to hospital only just in time, and now Professor Burden has a fatal accident. Isn't that news enough?"

"Yes." Mrs. Reid looked serious now. "It's very distressing. But I do assure you, Dr. Glenning, that before the Burdens came to live here, Whitelands was very much a quiet little backwater where really nothing ever happened."

"That's what the vicar said," remarked Paula thoughtfully. "What do you think, Mrs. Reid? Do you think Professor Burden's death was an accident?"

Mrs. Reid was quite equal to this sudden assault. In fact, she seemed pleased to have the chance of speaking her mind.

"Considering how much he was disliked around here," she said, "I should think it is perfectly possible that somebody pushed him over the edge. But it wasn't his wife. That I do know for sure, because she was at home watching television. I saw her."

"You saw her?"

They were approaching The Swan now, and Paula was feeling the need to be alone for a while, but this she had to stay and hear.

"How could you see her?" she asked. "You can't see into the sitting-room at The Twitten from the road."

"Oh, I didn't see into the room. I saw her come to the front door and call the cat. It was still very light. About a quarter to ten. I'd been at the vicarage. Glenys and I play piano duets now and then—very badly. But the vicar was out all evening, so he didn't suffer from our noise. I don't think Kitty Burden saw me," went on Mrs. Reid, forestalling another question from Paula, "and I didn't want to stop and chat. But I thought you would like to know, because I have a feeling—" She paused and then continued in a rush, "I've got a feeling that you might suspect her of making away with her husband, and I assure you that she didn't, and it's no kindness to her or to anybody else to come down here asking the sort of questions that might make people believe she did."

"But Mrs. Reid . . ." began Paula, very taken aback, very upset, and not at all sure what she was going to say.

"There. I've spoken out of turn. It isn't my business. I'm not really a close friend of any of them, except maybe Glenys. I don't really know Kitty Burden at all. She's not the sort of woman you can get to know easily, is she? Except that she always speaks very highly of you, so I suppose you must have— Well, anyway, that's what they tell me at the vicarage."

"I've got a great admiration for Kitty," said Paula. "I wish I could help her."

"Then go away," said Mrs. Reid unexpectedly firmly. "Get her to go with you if you can, but if not, then just go. It's not doing her any good to have you here. People are asking, 'Why should this inquisitive outsider—' Forgive me, Dr. Glenning. I know you mean well, but I don't think you quite understand. We used to be a very happy little community here, before the Burdens came, and now that the professor is dead, the sooner the widow is allowed to recover herself and then go away too— I'm sorry. I've said far too much. I must go. Goodbye."

She trotted off down the road, an odd little figure in the long, loose dress, leaving Paula feeling distressed and confused. Was it true that Kitty had such a high regard for her, she wondered as she walked through the seemingly deserted inn to the attic bedroom. Perhaps it was. There was the way Kitty had welcomed her earlier that afternoon and those talks in Paula's flat when Kitty came to stay; there was that first little meeting in Kitty's room upstairs, when she had confided in Paula. And, of course, the fact that Paula might well have saved her life when she found her unconscious from a mix of alcohol and drugs.

Had Kitty hoped for Paula's full trust and support, for a good friend who would not for one moment allow the suspicion to arise that she might have killed her husband?

If that was the case, then Paula had let her down very badly. Paula's mind went back to the uncomfortable conversation on the top of the chalk cliff, before returning again to Mrs. Reid's accusation that her very presence in the village was harming Kitty.

Paula sat down on the patchwork quilt that covered the bed, lit a cigarette, and stared unhappily out of the dormer window at an expanse of blue sky.

Six o'clock. Another hour and a half at least before James could be expected to arrive. Was she going to sit here miserably for all that time? But if I am such a menace, she asked herself, why didn't the vicar speak to me as Mrs. Reid has just done? Why did he more or less deliver Kitty into my hands? And in any case, since talking to Roger I have far more suspicions of him than I have of Kitty. What a pity they don't know that I have been talking to Roger.

"They." Who were "they?" Robert Fulham, Glenys Fulham, Mrs. Reid. Who else?

She got up and stood for a moment at the open window, looking along the village street. The gardens were as bright and attractive as ever; the church and its yew-trees made a pleasing contrast; the hills rising behind seemed sheltering, protective.

It was a snug little place. Paula suddenly remembered Louise Graverton, once a Londoner, saying that she had come to enjoy living here. A happy little community. The Burdens had been outsiders. And Paula herself was very much an outsider. It was an uncomfortable feeling. It was as if, behind those pretty gardens and casement windows, there was resentment and enmity.

"I'm getting fanciful," said Paula aloud to herself. "This is ridiculous. I shall go down and have a drink in the bar, and then I shall drive about and try to stop thinking about Whitelands."

She crushed out her cigarette carefully and with determination; was served a lager by the punk girl, silent and efficient as ever; and sat alone at one end of the saloon bar while at the other end a very young couple, obviously strangers to the place, whispered to each other and never glanced in her direction.

13

"Where on earth have you been?" asked James two hours later. "I'm starving, and if we don't hurry up, they're going to stop serving dinner."

Paula, looking flushed and rather out of breath, sat down opposite him in the corner of the tiny dining-room at The Swan.

"Oh— Order me anything," she said as James picked up the menu. "But no more to drink."

"Now," said James when his own wishes had been attended to. "Tell me all."

"The vicar was right," said Paula. "If you want to hear the local gossip, you've got to got to the Sussex Inn. It's horribly crowded and noisy, but I'm glad I went. I'd been driving around, you see, and I thought I'd have a look at the Woolf house at Rodmell, although of course it was too late to go in, but I thought I'd like to get the feel of the place and maybe walk along the path Virginia went along to drown herself. Yes, I know it sounds morbid, but I was feeling very depressed. Anyway, I didn't do it because they'd been having some sort of celebration in the village—a church fête or something—and the whole place was milling with cars and people carrying potted plants, and children with balloons, and a band playing. Yes, it was rather funny," added Paula as James began to laugh. "A most suitable corrective to my gloomy speculations. So I drove back to Whitelands, and I saw the Sussex Inn and thought I might as well go in and have a drink. Thank you."

This last was an acknowledgement of her grapefruit.

"I didn't see any faces I recognised," went on Paula, "but I got stuck in a corner where a group of people, mostly about sixty or older, were talking. They didn't take any notice of me, and they didn't care who heard what they said. It was about Bill Burden. I don't think they actually lived in Whitelands, but it must have been somewhere near, because they knew all about him and they knew about Roger and his precious Boyds and they also knew the Gravertons."

She swallowed a mouthful too hastily, nearly choked, and had to cough and drink water to recover.

"Henry Graverton," she went on a minute later, "was on a television show with Bill Burden a few years ago. "Mysteries of Modern Maths" or some such title. Not the sort of thing you or I would watch, but it was quite a popular series. This particular item was about statistics and economic forecasting, with Bill as the guru who knew everything and Henry down among the lower ranks who supplied the facts when asked to." Paula sipped at her water again. "Apparently he stepped out of line and dared to correct Bill on some minor calculation, and Bill was extremely offensive to him. It must have livened up the show, but according to the people in the pub, Henry has never forgiven him for this very public insult."

"In other words," concluded Paula, "the opinion of the regulars at the Sussex Inn is that Henry Graverton pushed Professor William Burden into the chalk-pit as a long-delayed act of revenge. There. What do you think of that, James?"

"I don't believe it," he said after a moment's thought.

"Why not?"

"It's not the way people get their own back. Not in the academic world. Suppose you wanted revenge for having been insulted in public. What would you do?"

"I don't know," said Paula thoughtfully. "If someone had given me a bad review, I'd be inclined to do the same to them when their next book was published. But that would only reach a limited audience if it was an academic book. This seems to have been a very wide audience, and we know only too well how offensive Bill could be. I rather like the idea of Henry sitting quietly at Bill's table and nursing his thoughts of revenge. And don't forget, he knows the terrain very well, wandering around in all weathers with his binoculars.''

"You're not suggesting that he isn't genuinely interested in birds and things?"

"Oh no. He's hooked on nature study. But he's also a bit hooked on Kitty. It could have been a sort of double motive."

"All right then. Include him in. What else have you been doing today?"

Paula told him throughout the rest of the meal and continued as they walked up the village street in the late-evening light.

As they came near to The Twitten, James interrupted her. "There are lights on in the house. Do you think Kitty is there? Shall we call?"

"I'd rather not," said Paula. "I think we'd best keep away." She had not yet told him of her encounter with Mrs. Reid and of the accusation that her presence in the village could be harmful to Kitty.

James still hesitated at the gate. "She needn't answer if she doesn't want to. Look—here's my feline friend."

He bent down and picked up the cat, which laid itself against his shoulder and purred loudly. "She remembers me. I'm going to ring the bell. You don't need to come if you don't want to."

"I don't want to. I think Kitty's had enough of me for today."

"See you later then."

James sounded very offhand. Paula, feeling a sudden return of the foreboding that she had felt during their first visit to the house, took a few steps up the garden path with him and said, "James, do wait a moment. Why are we here? I mean, why did we come?"

"To Whitelands, you mean? I thought we came because we are both dying to find out what's been happening and in particular to find the answer to the sixty-four thousand dollar question: Did she do it?"

"Didn't we want to try to help Kitty?"

"You did. You always have done. I can't say I feel so strongly about it. I suspect that Kitty is capable of helping herself."

Paula was scarcely listening to him. "It all seemed so different in London," she said. "It seemed quite harmless, our wanting to come. But since I've been here I've felt— Oh, James, suppose we are stirring things up? Suppose our being here means that somebody who thought he was safe feels threatened? Suppose our being here causes—"

"Another death?"

"Yes," said Paula miserably.

There was a silence. They stood half-way along the garden path, in the scented twilight. The air was very still. Then the cat began to wriggle and shot away into the bushes as soon as James let it go. At the same moment a light appeared in the porch.

Without speaking, James and Paula ran across the lawn to the side of the house that adjoined the twitten. Here they were in shadow and, with luck, would not be noticed.

Eavesdropping again, thought Paula; but we hadn't intended it.

Kitty came out of the house. They could see her clearly, just beyond the shelter of the porch, silhouetted against the broad shaft of light. She spoke to somebody. Her voice was low but clear.

"Thank you for coming. It's helped a lot to take it over. And I shall try to take your advice."

"Are you sure you won't come to us for the night?"

It was a man's voice, but they could not yet see the speaker. Robert Fulham? It might be, thought Paula.

"I wonder where that cat's got to," they heard Kitty say, and they held their breath, afraid that she was going to come out and search the garden.

"Enjoying her nocturnal prowl," said the man. "Why don't you let her stay out?"

"Because I don't want the doorstep littered with tiny corpses in the morning."

The man laughed. "You can't change animal nature. You shouldn't be so squeamish, Kit."

Definitely not the vicar, thought Paula, though a not dissimilar voice.

"I can't stand seeing anything dead. That's why I couldn't go on nursing."

"I know." The voice was very low and serious now. "I understand."

"And when I think of Louise finding Bill—"

"Don't think of it. Louise is tough. It was a shock, but she'll get over it."

Henry Graverton. Of course, said Paula to herself. James's slight movement beside her told her that he, too, had guessed who the speaker was.

"The trouble I've caused you," said Kitty.

"It's all over now. You'll go away, and we'll soon forget you both, you and Bill."

The man came out beyond the shelter of the porch and stood for a moment next to Kitty on the gravel path.

"Lovely night. I think I'll go for a stroll and startle the foxes."

"You do that, Henry," said Kitty as they took a few steps together. "I've never said this before, but I've often thought it: you really hated Bill, didn't you?"

"Yes, I hated him."

"You hid it very well."

"Needs must. He came to live here. It's my home. What else could I do but keep quiet and hope he would go away?"

Kitty did not respond.

"Well, goodnight then," they heard her say.

"Goodnight. I do wish you'd come to us if you're so afraid of him."

"Thanks again, but no. I'll lock up well."

They parted, and Kitty moved away onto the further lawn, out of the line of light. They could hear her calling. "Merry! Merry! Where are you, you bad cat?"

"Shall we make a dash for it?" whispered James.

"No. She'll see us."

But it looked as if they were bound to be discovered, once Kitty switched her search to the other side of the garden.

"Can't we get round to the back?" murmured Paula.

"No. There's this shed in the way. If we could climb the wall—"

"Ssh." Paula grabbed at him. "There's somebody coming. At the garden gate."

It was quite dark now, but their eyes had adjusted to the variations of shadow.

"Not Roger," whispered Paula. "Not big enough. It's—"

James gave her a warning nudge. They saw Kitty come once again into the shaft of light, saw the man who had come through the gate, saw the two silhouetted figures merge together and move towards the house. A moment later the porch light went out, and almost immediately after that there came a faint mew from the region of James's left foot.

"You're safe now, Merry," he said bending down. "You've won your night on the tiles."

"And we can go in peace." Paula spoke in her normal voice. "That was the Reverend Robert Fulham, vicar of this parish, and it doesn't look as if he's going to come away in a hurry."

"It looks as if you were right about his being Kitty's choice," said James when they were safely out of the garden and walking towards the churchyard. "I wonder what Glenys thinks about it all. Shall we go over to the vicarage and find out?"

"If you really mean that, then go by yourself," said Paula. "I told you—I'm not going to try to find out any more. In any case, it's too late for a social call."

"It won't be a social call. I shall be seeking spiritual guidance."

Paula laughed. She had not intended to sound unkind. In fact, the laugh was more in the nature of a release of tension than a response to James's remark, but it misfired completely.

"What's so funny?" he said very coldly. "Why should it always be assumed that I never need any comfort or help?"

"I didn't mean—" began Paula, and then stopped.

There was really nothing to say. The sudden opening up of a gulf between them was truly shocking. She had known in her heart, ever since their first visit to Whitelands, that the miseries of Kitty and Bill Burden were somehow or other going to spill over onto James and herself and ruin their own contentment. Either by luck or by care, they had managed to postpone the crisis until this moment. They had both wanted to know what was going to become of the Burdens, and this had kept them in harmony.

But now Bill was dead, and that had changed everything. It was as if all the resentment and hatred that had been focussed on him was now free-floating, seeking another object, weaving other patterns of human relationship that would satisfy the basic human need to hate.

And she and James had got caught up in this. If only she could convey these thoughts to him.

She tried to do so, walking beside him along the pathway between the yew-trees and the tombs. He heard her and she believed that he had taken in what she said and even agreed with it, but it did not bridge the gulf.

At the gate that led from the churchyard into the vicarage garden he stopped. He wanted her to leave him, but he did not say so. Had they been as they were before, trusting each other, he would have said so without any hesitation. But now they were estranged, and estrangement brought restrain and formality.

"Good luck," she said before turning back. "I hope you find what you're looking for."

"Thanks." James went through the gate and shut it between them. "I don't know when I'll be back. Don't stay up for me."

But the vicar isn't even there, thought Paula as she retraced her steps; he's with Kitty. There's only Glenys there. Glenys the comforter, in whom people confide, in whom Bill confided his own tragedy, the suicide of his mother.

She felt a little comforted herself as she thought of James talking to Glenys. It would do him good. Glenys Fulham was very much a man's woman, undemanding, softly manipulative, never really giving herself away. She could have done with a Glenys Fulham herself at this moment, but that was so often the fate of women—to have to be their own comforters.

Or to comfort each other.

At least she had been of some help to Kitty, thought Paula as she reached the top of the churchyard mound and stood for a moment a few feet away from the church porch. But then she had failed her. Instead of believing totally in Kitty's innocence, she had suspected Kitty of killing her husband. Did Robert Fulham suspect? Did he perhaps know? Hate the sin but love the sinner—that sort of thing.

Paula looked around her. The churchyard was full of shadows. The nearest human light was the street lamp near to the lych-gate. Further down the village street were lamps and lighted windows, and looking back the way she had come, she could just see the porch light of the vicarage between the trees. She could not see any lights in the windows of The Twitten to her right: the yew-trees blocked the view.

Supposing Kitty and Robert really want to marry, she thought, what are they going to do? There is Glenys, who, with all her virtues and her self-command, will not take kindly to being replaced by a wife at the vicarage. And then there is Roger, disappointed in his dearest hopes and steaming with revenge.

And Philip. Would he be disappointed too?

She was glad to leave the churchyard. The quarrel—if it could be called a quarrel—with James had made her feel very much alone. She sat down for a while on the wooden seat under the lych-gate and tried to decide what to do next. She was tired, but the prospect of returning to the inn held no appeal. Much more attractive was the notion of driving back to London and hiding away in her own little nest, where loneliness was eased out by snugness and familiarity.

Why not? It would be very late by the time she got back, but the weekend lay ahead and she could sleep as long as she liked. Of course, she would leave a note for James: this was not intended to be an anxiety-raising disappearance. Let him solve the mystery on his own, if there was indeed a mystery to solve, and return to London to tell her about it, and then they would shake down into their normal lives once more.

"I'm going to do just that," Paula said aloud and got to her feet.

But she had only walked a short distance into the roadway when she heard footsteps behind her. She had time for the fear and the apprehension, the shortening of the breath and the tensing of the muscles that accompany the awareness of being followed in the darkness, before she heard the voice.

"It's Paula Glenning, isn't it?"

A man's voice, faintly familiar, slightly out of breath.

"Philip? Sorry. I wasn't running away. I was deep in thought."

"I'm sorry to interrupt you," he said, "but I'm dreadfully worried and I thought perhaps you might have— Paula, have you seen my father?"

"I saw him earlier this afternoon."

"Yes, I know. Or rather, I guessed it must be you, although he said— But I didn't mean then; I meant just now."

Paula was puzzled by his incoherence. She remembered him as competent and self-assured almost to a fault.

"No, I've not seen him," she replied. "James and I have been walking over to the vicarage, and I've left him there and am going back to The Swan."

"You came through the churchyard?"

"Yes. It's very dark up there. If he's there, I could easily have missed him."

And thank heaven for that, thought Paula as she was speaking; one wouldn't want to encounter crazy Roger in the darkness.

"Do you think he is in the churchyard?" she added.

"I don't know," said Philip hopelessly. Then he seemed to make an effort to take command of himself. "I'm sorry to have troubled you. My father has lapses of memory from time to time, and I am always rather anxious when he is out late at night. I'll look around a bit more, and if I can't find him, I'll just have to go home and wait."

"Are you thinking," asked Paula tentatively, "that he might have come out to see Kitty Burden?"

They both turned and looked across at Kitty's house. The porch light was now on, and several of the windows showed light behind the curtains. Was Robert still there, wondered Paula. Was Kitty still there, or had they both fled? And if so, to where?

The house looked very peaceful, not at all as if it had been subjected to an assault by Philip's father.

"That might have been his intention," Philip was saying. "That's what is worrying me."

"But Kitty won't let him in," said Paula reassuringly. She would have liked to add that she didn't think Kitty was alone, but felt it would not be tactful to mention Robert Fulham at the moment.

"I hope she won't," said Philip. "I do wish I knew where he had gone."

"Could he have gone up to the top of the hill?" asked Paula.

Half of her was still longing to get away from the village and back to her own life: the other half contained a mixture of genuine feeling for Philip and a reawakened curiosity about his father's part in the Whitelands affair.

"We might have," muttered Philip, and then hastily added, "He might have gone anywhere."

"Let's try the hill path first," said Paula with determination. "It seems to be quite a favourite evening walk. Come on."

And she set off along the narrow alleyway between Kitty's garden wall and the churchyard, glad of something to occupy her mind, grateful to have something to do that was not quite so drastic as abandoning James and returning alone to London, but at the same time wondering whether it was wise to approach the danger spot alone with Philip in the darkness, for it seemed plain enough that he suspected his father of causing the accident to Bill, and if he also suspected that Paula had found a means of proving this . . .

It was better not to think about it. She had made her choice and there was to be no escaping from Whitelands until the whole business had reached some sort of resolution.

14

It was very dark at the lower end of the path beneath the trees.

"I'll go first," said Philip. "I've got a flashlight." And a moment later. "It's very good of you to come, Paula. I didn't mean to drag you up here, but I'm very glad to have company. Particularly the company of somebody who really understands about my father, as I believe you do."

"My father and mother both died when I was very young," said Paula, "so I don't have a parent problem, but many of my friends and colleagues do. It must be very painful to watch them failing."

"It is. And even worse when it's the mind that's going, and not the body."

"Yes indeed. You must lose all contact; you lose the person."

They walked on in silence. We must be nearly at the bottom of the chalk-pit, thought Paula when Philip paused to flash the light over a tangle of brambles and gorse bushes at the left of the path.

"This is where we found Bill. Or rather, where Louise found him. Henry and I were further up the hill when we heard her shouting. Poor old Louise."

Paula said nothing. It seemed better not to admit that she had already been over the ground with Kitty that afternoon. Let Philip tell the tale in his own way.

"It's terribly overgrown," he went on, "but there is a way through somewhere to the clearer bit at the foot of the cliff."

"You think your father might have come here?" asked Paula.

"Does he get confused abut which day it is? I mean, could he be thinking you were still looking for Bill, as you were last night?"

"It's not impossible." Philip was pushing aside the brambles. "He's very muddled sometimes. We can get through here. Careful!"

Paula pushed her way through, glad that she was wearing trousers and a long-sleeved jacket. Philip doesn't know the ground as well as Kitty does, she thought: this afternoon we found an easier way.

"Oughtn't we to try calling your father?" she suggested when they had reached the comparatively clear patch near the cliff.

"Yes, of course. Is there anybody here?" Philip raised his voice and flashed the light around.

He called again. The light moved further away from the spot where Paula was standing. She had a moment of panic when it seemed as if Philip was going to disappear completely. The thought of making her own way back in the dark was very unpleasant, but at the same time she was still not quite sure that he wasn't putting on an act for her benefit. He certainly seemed worried enough, and judging from her own limited knowledge of Roger, he probably had good cause to be; nevertheless she could not quite stifle her suspicion of him.

"I don't think he can be here," said Philip, returning from his exploration. "The cliff goes quite a long way round, and after that there's a thicket that only rabbits can get through. I oughtn't to have brought you, Paula. It's very selfish of me. I'd better light you back to the village."

"Don't you want to go on searching?"

"Yes, but it's not fair to expect you to come too."

"I don't mind. I've nothing else to do. And I like your father."

"We'll go on then. But we have to be careful. We don't want any more accidents."

A little later he added, "It gets rather steep here. My father knows every stone of this path and of all the others around. I'm afraid I'm not so familiar with them. Do take care. Can you see enough?"

"Yes, thanks."

Paula was bending down and using her hands to help scramble up the slope. They came out, catching their breath, onto the open grassy hillside.

"I'm out of condition," said Philip. "I ought to do something about it. Coo-ee! Anyone about?"

He switched off the light and stood calling. There was no response.

Paula was looking at the stars. The air was soft and pure and still.

"I can see why people come up here for their evening walk," she said when Philip was silent again.

"It's not my sort of thing," he replied abruptly, "and I'm beginning to feel that I've had enough. We can't walk the whole of the South Downs Way at this time of night in search of him. Shall we go back?"

"Perhaps he might have gone to the place where Bill fell," suggested Paula. "It was somewhere up here, wasn't it?" she added hastily.

"He'd have heard me calling," said Philip. "It's only a few yards away, past those bushes." He switched on the light again. "There's a most inadequate warning and protection, and I don't think it's wise to wander about there in the dark. In fact, I very nearly went over the bloody cliff myself when we were looking for Bill last night."

Paula murmured sympathetically. Having decided that their excursion was in fact just what it seemed—a search for Roger—and that Philip intended her no harm, she had felt at the same time relief and a sense of anticlimax. But if he was going to speak of his own volition about Bill's death, then she had no objection to hearing. It might be interesting. She would not try any further investigations, but if somebody actually started talking to her, that was different.

"Yes, it was most unpleasant," said Philip as they began to retrace their steps along the easy slope that preceded the steep section of the path. "Henry and I were up here, shouting for Bill just as I've been doing for my father, and since Henry knows the area well and I don't, I just followed him. We both had flashlights, of course, but I was focussing mine straight ahead and had no idea that the bushes to my left were at the very edge of the cliff. It was only when I felt the ground actually moving that I realised and quickly moved away."

He paused, and Paula, reflecting that she had had a very similar experience that afternoon, once again expressed suitable concern.

"I caught my foot on a bramble and only just missed falling headlong into a blackberry bush," went on Philip. "That's how I came to see the brooch. Kitty's brooch. You've probably noticed her wearing it. A little enamel oval with a scroll design in various shades of blue. It isn't valuable, but it belonged to her mother and she is very fond of it."

"Yes, I remember it," said Paula, hoping that her eagerness was not too evident in her voice. Although he wouldn't be telling me this, she thought, if he didn't want me to know, if he didn't want me to draw the obvious conclusion.

They reached the steep slope again and for the next few minutes were fully occupied in making a safe descent. Then Philip began to talk again.

"You can imagine how I felt when I found this brooch. If I hadn't slipped and had to bend down to save myself, I would never have noticed it, but somebody else would have found it. The police, no doubt, when they looked around this morning."

"Yes," said Paula with forced calm. And then, because it was not natural to show no reaction to his story and because she could see no reason why she should pretend to be unaffected by it, she added with much more feeling, "Oh Philip, what a shock for you! What did you do?"

"Pocketed it. And there it is still. I haven't told a soul about it. Not until this moment."

"You haven't told Kitty you found it up there?"

"I haven't had the chance. There's not been a single moment when I could speak to her alone."

"Not even last night, when she stayed with you at Boyds?"

"Last night," said Philip, "she was dead to the world with the effects of a sleeping-drug. Even then I had great difficulty in preventing my father from trying to wake her in the early hours of the morning. When eventually she did wake up, he would not leave her alone for a second. It was a great relief to me when the vicar came and spirited her away. Since then, I have had to go to London, and I got back this evening to find no sign of my father. I then came out and found you."

"Kitty will know the brooch is missing," began Paula.

"That is moderately obvious," broke in Philip, shining the light for her so that she could avoid the tree-roots at the lower part of the path. "She must be going quite crazy, wondering where it is."

"She was going crazy," exclaimed Paula. "That explains a lot. She must have been looking for it. I ought to have told you, Philip."

And she went on to explain about her talk with Kitty and their walk up the hill that afternoon.

"I had a feeling that she was looking for something in the gorse bushes," she concluded, "when she was chattering about specimens of wild flowers."

"That's it," said Philip. "Of course, she can't be sure she dropped it there, and of course, she didn't want to be caught up there on her own, searching. That would look suspicious. She's probably still hoping that she'll find it in the garden at her house. Or even over at Boyds. She certainly won't feel safe until she knows where it is."

"You were going to give it back to her?"

"Of course. What else?"

"And tell her where you found it?"

"That I had not quite decided. I wouldn't want her to think that I was holding this knowledge over her as any sort of threat. Of course, it links her strongly with Bill's accident, but it by no means proves that she pushed him over. On the other hand, I very much dislike telling lies. You may think that odd, coming from a lawyer, but it is a fact. Possibly a reaction against the fantasy world of my father. He has always found it difficult to adjust to reality, even before his memory began to fail."

They reached the end of the path and stood still under the lamp by the entrance to the churchyard.

"Why do you tell me this?" asked Paula in a low voice. "Why should you trust me? For all you know, I might go straight to the police."

"I suppose," said Philip after a moment's reflection, "that some part of me is hoping that you will. I can't do it myself. I don't know what to do. I am absolutely torn in two. In loyalty to Kitty I ought to keep quiet, but Bill was my friend as well. Shall we sit down for a moment?"

Paula led the way to the wooden seat in the lych-gate where she had sat not much more than half an hour earlier with very different thoughts and feelings.

"You see, I am very weak," said Philip unhappily. "I need to share the burden. I can't share it with anybody here. You are an outsider, but I believe you know as much about it as anybody. In my position, Paula, what would you do?"

"Probably just what you've done. Try to find somebody else to give me some advice."

"Thank you," he laughed shortly. "Then I'm not alone in my weakness."

"Don't you think," said Paula presently, "that whatever we decide to do, Kitty ought to be told where you found the brooch and given a chance to explain how it came to be there?"

"Naturally," replied Philip in a voice whose sarcastic over-tones failed to conceal the unhappiness underneath, "the correct procedure must be followed. The appropriate warning must be given. Anything you say may be used in evidence, and so on. You are entitled to keep silent until you have consulted your lawyer—who, incidentally, happens to be me."

"What a horrible position!" said Paula. "I'm only on the fringes of this, but I've been feeling quite sorry for myself that I'm involved at all."

"The other alternative," continued Philip as if she had not spoken, "assuming that the fall was not an accident, is also somebody very close to me."

"Your father," said Paula in a low voice, since this time he was obviously hoping that she would speak.

"My father," repeated Philip flatly. "You've seen enough of him to realise what he is like."

"Do you know where he was at the time Bill fell?"

"He'd been seen going up the path to the chalk-pit."

"I know. Kitty told me she had seen him. But if she was up there herself, either before or after—"

"Kitty tells lies," said Philip heavily. "She does it intentionally. My father tells lies, but he believes in them."

"Suppose they were both of them involved. Not by pre-arrangement," went on Paula hastily, "but by chance."

"I have supposed it." Philip leaned forward and rested his head on his hands. "I've supposed every possibility. There's no way out. I have to pass it all over to the proper authorities. Thank you for helping me to make up my mind." He stood up. "I'll talk to Kitty tonight. There's no point in trying to talk to my father, but I do wish I knew where he was."

"And I wish I could help. I'm going to wait here a little longer. If I should see him—" Paula broke off and got to her feet as well. "What's that noise?" she added.

Somewhere in the distance somebody was shouting. Philip looked towards The Twitten. "I think it's coming from the other direction," said Paula, starting off up the path through the churchyard.

Philip followed her. The noise increased. There seemed to be at least two men's voices involved, possibly other voices as well. It sounds just like a fight outside a pub, thought Paula; most inappropriate in a churchyard.

With the help of Philip's flashlight, their progress was quick. When they came to the way down to the vicarage, Philip exclaimed, "It's my father. I thought so."

"And the vicar? Oh no! My God, it's James! Oh no. This is absurd. Absurd."

Paula was running forward, stumbling and crying out.

"Stop it! Stop it, you fools!"

They were inside the churchyard, some distance from the vicarage gate but dimly visible in the light of the lamp by the gate. There was a howl of rage or of pain, and one of the flailing figures dropped backwards towards a low tombstone.

A woman's voice cried, "Stop it!" in much the same tone as Paula had used.

Philip ran forward and knelt down on the grass beside the man who had fallen.

"He's hit his head on the marble," he said. "We must get him to hospital."

"I'll call the ambulance," Glenys Fulham said and disappeared in the direction of the vicarage.

"Have you gone mad?" yelled Paula to James, who was leaning against a neighbouring gravestone and nursing his jaw.

"I haven't," he replied indignantly and then groaned as if it hurt him to speak. "But the old man has. He's gone berserk. I came out of the gate, and he came out from behind a holly bush and went for me. I'm very sorry." He roused himself with an effort and came towards Philip. "Honestly I was only trying to protect myself."

"I know." Philip stood up. "It's not your fault. He's done this sort of thing before. I'm sorry you had to get involved."

"D'you think he's badly hurt?"

"It looks as if he's concussed, but no doubt he'll recover."

Philip sounded infinitely weary. "That isn't for the first time either."

"I'm sorry," said James again. He sounded very subdued and completely sincere, and Paula was glad that he refrained from his usual habit of extended apologies and self-justifications. "What I can't understand," he went on, "is why he should attack me. I hadn't even spoken to him. I'd been having a chat with Glenys and was coming back through the churchyard to see if Paula was still around or had gone back to The Swan, and suddenly this whirlwind appeared and nearly knocked me out. Why me? What have I done to him?"

"Nothing," said Philip in a tight, unhappy voice. "If you want to make a charge for assault—"

"Oh, don't be absurd!" cried Paula before James could speak. "Of course we understand about your father. I've got it!" she went on excitedly. "He mistook you for somebody else."

"Coming out of the vicarage . . ." began James slowly. And then, with a sudden movement that caused him to wince and rub his jaw again, "The vicar! He must have thought I was the vicar. What do you think, Paula?"

"It sounds quite possible. You're taller than Robert Fulham, but the light's not good, and if Roger was expecting the vicar— Do you agree, Philip?"

"I think that's very likely what happened."

"I'm glad it wasn't meant for me," said James, "but I really don't see why he should attack the vicar either."

"Tell you later," said Paula, thinking that James's own reasoning must have been somewhat affected by the battering he had received if he had forgotten how Roger Aston's own hopes had been dashed by the vicar's annexation of Kitty.

Philip crouched down beside his father again, and there followed a rather awkward silence, broken at last by the return of Glenys with a blanket and the welcome news that the ambulance would not be long.

"We're to keep him warm," she said, "and James, I think

you'd better come back to the house and I'll find something to put on that bruise. Would you like to come too, Paula? I expect Philip will prefer to remain here."

Wonderful Glenys, thought Paula as she and James meekly followed her through the vicarage garden. I wonder what advice she will give to Philip in his dilemma.

15

"Much better," murmured James the next morning in reply to Paula's enquiry as the the state of his jaw. "That stuff Glenys put on it has worked wonders."

"I'll go down and get them to fix you a breakfast tray," said Paula.

"I'd rather come down. Do I look all right?"

"A trifle battered, but you'll pass. Don't hurry, darling. I want to phone Philip and find out how Roger is."

"You do that. I'm sorry about all this."

"All this" was clearly meant to include their yesterday's estrangement as well as the fight. Paula stopped in the doorway, smiled, and raised her hand. "I won't be long."

Philip answered the phone at once. "My father seems to be improving," he said. "It takes more than a marble gravestone to kill him. Tell James not to worry. How is he?"

"Fine."

"That's a comfort at any rate. And yourself?"

"Slept like a log. Philip . . ." Paula said with some hesitation, "I don't know if you'd rather forget about our talk yesterday evening. If so and if you want me to forget it, I'll try to do so. I haven't yet told James. But I can't help wondering—"

"About my problem. Yes. I did manage to have a word with her last night. I'd rather not explain on the phone, but perhaps you'd like to drop in at Boyds for coffee later this morning. I shan't be going to London today. I don't know what your own plans are."

"Neither do we, but we'll certainly come along for coffee."

James did not sound very enthusiastic about this suggestion. "You go on your own," he said to Paula when they were eating a leisurely breakfast in the dining-room of The Swan. "Philip and I don't mix. He'll be much happier without me there, and so will you."

"But what are you going to do?"

"I haven't yet decided. Perhaps I'll go and report on my state of health to Glenys. I might learn something of interest at the vicarage."

"You're not still trying to find out—"

"Aren't you?"

They stared at each other and then began to laugh.

"I really did mean to leave it alone," said Paula.

"I know you did, but you can't. It's not in your nature. Shall we meet back here at one o'clock at the bar and report on our progress?"

Paula agreed. "And please don't get into any more fights," she added. "I do rather care what happens to you."

"I echo your sentiments. Don't forget that you will be alone in that great house with a possible suspect."

"Not Philip."

"Why not?"

"Because— Oh, it's no use. I'll have to tell you. I'm not breaking any confidences. He'll expect me to. I'll be as quick as I can."

When Paula had finished, James said, "Did he actually show you the brooch?"

"No."

"But you believed him?"

"Of course I believed him. You'd have believed him in the circumstances."

"There wouldn't have been such circumstances. Philip and I are antipathetic. I thought you didn't like him either."

"I don't like him, but I couldn't help seeing that he was in a very difficult position."

"If it was true, yes, he was."

"It must be true," said Paula. "It could be too easily disproved. Kitty would only have to produce the brooch."

"He might have found it somewhere else."

"That's possible," said Paula grudgingly. "Okay. Philip's still a suspect. Why should he want Bill out of the way? He doesn't want to marry Kitty, and his father is going to be more nuisance about it than ever if Bill isn't there. I don't see any motive for Philip at all."

"Neither do I at the moment," admitted James. "But there's a very great deal that we don't know about all these people. Money, for instance. Kitty needs it badly. Roger and Philip need it badly. Bill had got it. And if Philip is handling Kitty's affairs, then presumable he was handling Bill's as well. Maybe he was mishandling them."

"You're not going to suggest that Philip murdered Bill to stop him finding out that Philip had been embezzling?"

"It's happened before. It's not impossible."

"I don't believe it. I'm going to ask him myself," said Paula, getting up from the table.

"Then I shall come with you after all if you are going to be so rash. The vicarage can wait. But first of all I'd like to see that chalk-pit. Could you face a third visit there? If not, then I'll go by myself."

"I think we'd better stick together," said Paula. "You might get attacked again."

But they encountered nobody on the hillside except a couple of walkers and a young man examining the broken fence and looking with distaste at the prickly bushes with which it was surrounded.

"Awkward sort of repair job," remarked James.

The young man produced a measuring rod and made no reply.

"Why does there always have to be a death before they repair a road or remove a hazard," remarked James as he and Paula walked away.

"Because it has to go through a committee."

"And why didn't Bill turn his energies to getting this place made safe instead of trying to stop the road-works?"

"Because it's only a boring and necessary little local job and can't be presented as a noble environmental campaign. Hurry up, James. We're going to be late."

They reached Boyds shortly after eleven. Philip came to the door, informed them that his father was going on as well as could be expected, and then led them not along the corridor to the breakfast-room but in the other direction, to what appeared to be the main reception-room of the house.

It was beautifully proportioned, with long windows and moulded ceilings, but there were marks on the shabby wallpaper where pictures had been removed, and the furnishings consisted of battered armchairs and a couple of cheap and shiny new coffee-tables. The most surprising thing about the room, however, was that it seemed to be full of people. Henry Graverton got up from one of the ancient chairs as they entered, and Louise called out a greeting.

"Philip never told me there was to be a gathering of the clans," said Paula, coming forward and greeting Robert and Glenys Fulham as well.

"I'll help Kitty with the coffee," Philip said and left the room.

"Are you feeling better this morning?" Glenys asked James.

"Fine. And I gather Roger is improving." James seated himself next to her.

"So Kitty is here too." Paula turned to Henry. "Do you know what this is all about?"

"I think we had better wait for Philip," he replied with a glance at his wife, and Paula was reminded of the first time they had met.

"Don't look so alarmed," said Robert Fulham, who was sitting the other side of her, "there's nothing sinister about this meeting. Very much the contrary, in fact."

Glenys was talking to James. "It's all Robert's doing. He's persuaded Kitty to come forward and clear the air. It wasn't fair on Philip, it wasn't fair on any of us to let us go on wondering and speculating."

"You can say that again," said Louise.

"My dear," protested Henry, "hadn't we better wait for the others before we start discussing it?"

Louise shrugged. "Oh well. If you insist on this farce."

"It's Kitty who wanted it this way."

"And Kitty's wish is law. Personally I can't see why she and Philip couldn't have just explained to Paula and James on the quiet instead of dragging us in. I can't really spare the time. I've got proofs to correct."

Paula looked at Louise with some sympathy. She looked tired and worried and old. Something has gone wrong in that marriage, thought Paula, and it's never going to be quite the same again. And it had been Louise who actually found Bill's body, she remembered. That must have been a most unpleasant experience, but nobody seemed to be at all concerned about Louise. She was tough; she could take it.

Poor Louise. No wonder she was so jealous of Kitty.

It was a relief when the door opened and Philip came in carrying a tray, followed by Kitty with another.

Which of the many facets of Kitty would she be presenting now, wondered Paula as she looked up at her. Judging by appearances, it was certainly not the well-groomed hostess, for Kitty was wearing some threadbare corduroy trousers and a white shirt that needed ironing, and Paula, in her most casual clothes, looked quite elegant in comparison.

But neither was it the sick and shabby woman who had visited the psychiatric clinic in Hampstead and stayed with Paula in her London flat, for on Kitty's face was an expression of triumph, of contentment, almost of joy.

There was no mistaking it. At this moment she was the calmest, the happiest person in the room. All the others were suffering in varying degrees from agitation and impatience. Even Glenys Fulham's rather smug self-composure appeared to be wearing thin. Her brother appeared exhausted; the Gravertons seemed restless and irritable; and Philip, who was dispensing the coffee, looked worst of all.

"This wasn't intended," he said to Paula as he handed her a cup, "but the situation has changed since I spoke to you this morning."

"Your father?" she asked.

"He's on the mend. They've no doubt that he is going to recover—physically, at any rate. Unfortunately his mind looks like being more confused than ever."

"I'm sorry," said Paula. "I'm truly sorry."

"And so am I," said James. "I can't help feeling responsible."

Philip gave a faint shrug, as if it would tire him too much to respond. "Is everybody served?" he asked, looking round. "All right, then, Kitty. The floor is yours."

He sat down in a very old but comfortable-looking armchair rather apart from the rest of the group, leaned back, and shut his eyes.

"Poor old Phil," said Kitty, glancing at him. "He's having a rough time, and it's partly my fault. In fact, I've really asked him to arrange this get-together so that I could apologise to you all. It won't take long. Thank you for coming."

She sat down on the broad arm of Robert's chair and took a drink of coffee.

"As you probably all know, I haven't been telling the truth about my part in Bill's death. Robert has been spending hours trying to persuade me to come clean, but I couldn't face it."

This isn't going to be a confession, Paula told herself; this is Kitty at her most mocking, her most mischievous.

Kitty's next remark bore this out.

"Sorry, folks, but this isn't a confession. I didn't do it, but I know who almost certainly did, and I wasn't going to say anything, since the police were convinced that it was an accident and it seemed best to leave it that way. Two things have made me change my mind."

She glanced at Philip, who appeared to be asleep.

"Phil knows about it already," she went on. "We went over it all again early this morning after he'd had the hospital report on Roger. Let him sleep. He's had enough of me and my problems, but it's all over now."

"I thought you were going to be quick," said Louise irritably. "What are the two things that made you change your mind?"

"My losing my brooch, and Roger getting a knock on the head."

"Hurry up then," snapped Louise. "We can't wait all day."

"I saw Roger go up the hill path," went on Kitty after an amused glance at Louise, "about an hour after Bill had gone that way. My television programme was over and it was a lovely evening and I decided to have a walk as well. There was still some light in the sky when I got to the top. I couldn't see Bill anywhere, but I saw Roger. He was coming away from the place where the fence is broken and he looked very excited. He was waving his arms and shouting. I couldn't hear any of the words. It was rather scary, and I stepped behind a tree and hoped he wouldn't notice me, which he didn't, but he came within a couple of feet of me and I heard what he was saying. It was 'Got the bugger'—or something like that. He went off down the path, and when I thought it was safe, I came out and switched on my flashlight and decided to try to find out what Roger had been up to.

"I came nearer to the broken fence. I know all about it, and I was very careful, but I couldn't see anything different from the last time I'd been up there. It must have been when I was pushing my way between bramble bushes that I lost my brooch.

"I didn't notice it at the time. Not until the next morning, as a matter of fact. It was pinned to the front of my dress; it wasn't holding anything together. When I got back and found Bill hadn't returned, I began to feel worried. That's when I called round to everyone and you organised a search-party. You know the rest."

Kitty stopped abruptly, twisted herself round on the arm of the vicar's chair, smiled down at him, and asked, "Have I said enough? Have I done what you wanted, Robert?"

"Yes. I'll take over now." Robert Fulham did not respond to her smile. His voice was without emotion as he continued. "Kitty believes that Roger had just pushed Bill over the cliff when she saw and heard him. She didn't want Philip to know and she thought the best thing was to keep quiet about it. I disagreed. I felt that Philip had the right to know, and eventually she said that she would only come forward with this story if somebody was actually suspected of killing her husband.

"This is exactly what happened. Philip, finding Kitty's brooch, began to have suspicions of Kitty herself. The position now is that all of us present in this room know that there is a strong possibility that Roger Aston killed Bill Burden. Nobody outside this room has this knowledge, although no doubt others have their suspicions."

"So you want us to promise to keep quiet," said James, who had for some time been showing signs of wishing to interrupt.

"I'm not asking anything. I'm putting the facts to you," said the vicar.

"I don't see any point in involving the old man," said Henry. "We're not even sure about it, and he's sick and confused."

"That's true," said Paula, "but on the other hand—" She looked across at Philip. His eyes were still closed and he did not move. "What does Philip think?" she asked.

Kitty got up and moved over to Philip's chair.

"Phil needs all our help and care and support," she said, sitting down and laying a protective arm on Philip's shoulder. "I don't think he should be asked to decide on anything until he's had a chance to sleep on it."

There were murmurs of assent from the three other men present. Paula kept quiet, but Louise Graverton, turning in Kitty's direction, said very nastily, "Until you've had a chance to work on him, you mean." Then she turned back and addressed the room at large. "How do we know that Kitty is not making all this up to cover herself?"

This produced protests all round, including one from Glenys, and Philip roused himself to speak. "She's not making it up. I could give you reasons for this statement, but it would involve saying things about my father that I would rather not say."

"We're not asking you to," said Henry. "Don't take any notice of Louise."

James and Robert made similar remarks. Glenys looked a little disturbed, and Paula sat silent, noting Kitty's look of satisfaction. Louise, clearly defeated, said, "Oh no, don't take any notice of me. I'm in a minority of one. Naturally I have to accept the will of the majority. You needn't worry. I won't let you down. I'll stick to my brief at the inquest."

There was an uncomfortable silence after she had finished speaking. Her hurt feelings filled the room, and nobody made any move to console her.

Louise stood up and turned to Philip. "Have you got a usable bathroom anywhere in this mausoleum of yours?"

"Yes. I'll show you."

Philip sounded pleased to have an excuse to move.

"I'll come too if I may," said Paula.

She wanted to get away from that look on Kitty's face. But you thought you wanted to see the real Kitty behind all the different acts, she said to herself, and now you've seen it you don't like it at all. Mocking and merciless, no genuine feeling for anybody. Except, of course, for the poor idiot daughter.

And perhaps for Robert.

They were following Philip up a narrow staircase. "Servants quarters," he murmured apologetically. "We live in this end of the house. Smaller rooms, easier to heat. Here's the bathroom; here's the loo. Can you find your way back?"

"Yes, thanks," said Louise and Paula almost in one voice.

"I'm not going to wait for Henry," said Louise after Philip had left them. "He can do what he likes. Would you mind telling him that I've gone straight home?"

"Of course I will," said Paula.

After that neither of them spoke another word. Paula was glad of this. She believed that she and Louise were thinking along very much the same lines at the moment and that it was better for their thoughts to remain unspoken. Louise must repair her damaged marriage as best she could, and as for Paula herself, she must smile and utter polite insincerities and wish Kitty a happier future and hope that James would not linger too long in his farewells.

16

"The inquest," said Paula a week later. "Isn't it today? This is the last of my marmalade," she added. "I'll make some more next year."

The summer vacation had begun, and they were enjoying an unhurried breakfast at James's flat.

"The inquest was yesterday," said James. "There ought to be a mention of it in *The Times*. Get down, Rosie."

He dropped the newspaper in order to attend to the black cat, which was trying to get onto the table.

Paula picked up the crumpled sheets and began to look through them. "Here it is. Professor William Burden, etc., etc. Verdict of accidental death."

"All according to plan."

"She killed him, James."

"Very likely. Stop it, you greedy cat. All right then—you can have some bacon."

"And she'd got away with it," said Paula. "I wonder what will happen now. Will Robert Fulham marry her?"

"No," said James very decisively.

"How do you know?"

"Because his sister says he won't."

"You never told me you talked about it to Glenys," said Paula reproachfully.

"I'm telling you now. People do confide in me, you know. Glenys said that her brother was deeply in love with Kitty Burden and she was very worried about him because it wasn't making him happy. Kitty seemed to care for him, but he felt he couldn't trust her."

"I suppose he must have suspected all along that she was guilty. What will she do? Will she leave Whitelands?"

James had reorganised *The Times* and did not answer.

"You could call Glenys as you're such good friends with her," said Paula, "and find out."

"And you could call your friend Philip."

There was a silence while James read and Paula made a great fuss of the cat. At last James got up and went into the living-room. Paula, feeling very virtuous and self-controlled, remained at the breakfast-table.

"Lot of movement going on down in Sussex," he said when he returned. "The Gravertons went off straight after the inquest to have a look at Norway and the midnight sun, and Robert has been persuaded by his boss, the bishop, to take a holiday. They are getting a locum in, and Glenys is taking him to the Scilly Isles to look at the flowers and lie in the sun."

"What about Roger? Is he out of hospital?"

"Coming out tomorrow. A convalescent home has been advised, and Philip is driving him to Bournemouth and then having a break himself. Glenys doesn't know where he is going."

"And Kitty?"

"Kitty seems to have done a good job in depopulating Whitelands. She has now removed herself to a small rented cottage within walking distance of Mrs. Matthews and Marie, and has taken her few personal possessions with her. Philip has instructions to sell the house and dispose of the rest of its contents as soon as possible. Mrs. Reid, the pottery lady, is giving a home to the cat. I think that's about all."

"And Bill's funeral?"

"That's this afternoon. Very quiet. At Brighton crematorium. There will be a university memorial service later on in London with all the full works."

"Shall you go to it?"

"Yes. After all, he was a sort of friend."

A sort of friend, said Paula to herself, imagining the words inscribed as an epitaph on a tombstone. What a lukewarm tribute at the close of a human life.

But at least it was sincere, which was more than could be said for the tributes at the memorial service a couple of weeks later. Paula accompanied James, not because she particularly wanted to go but because she had a nagging sense of incompleteness, of dissatisfaction, whenever she thought of the Whitelands affair, and she had a rather forlorn hope that the service might somehow help to round the whole business off.

She came away from the church deeply depressed. The proceedings, organised by Professor Burden's former colleagues, had been very well conducted but totally lacking in feeling. Everybody said the right things and nobody really cared. No one from Whitelands was there except Glenys, and she came in at the very last moment and disappeared before they had a chance to speak to her.

"Kitty ought to have come," said Paula to James when they were driving away. "I don't care what she's done or what she feels like, she ought to have been there putting on a decent act. It wouldn't have hurt her. She's very good at it."

"I thought I saw Bill's first wife, Greta," said James. "Somewhere at the back."

"There you are then. If she could make the gesture, why couldn't Kitty? It's . . . it's unnecessarily unkind. It's discourteous."

"I'm surprised you care about such things," said James. "I didn't know you condoned hypocrisy."

Paula did not reply. She was in fact rather surprised herself at the strength of her own reactions.

Every now and then during the course of the next six months, one or the other of them would happen to mention Bill or Kitty

Burden, but neither of them made any attempt to get in touch
with any of the Whitelands people, and when they had occasion
to drive down to Sussex, they deliberately avoided going anywhere near the village.

Marmalade-making time had come round again, and it was a
year, almost to the day, after that first snowbound visit that Paula
received a picture postcard from Kitty.

The view was of the Statue of Liberty, but the postmark was
San Francisco.

"Marie died," wrote Kitty, "and I'm going slowly round the
world. Do you remember saying that, in the event of a certain
contingency, you would have got up and gone right out of my
life for ever? Well, I've done it instead. Be happy, Paula. Goodbye."

"What does she mean?" asked James. "When did you say
that? What was the contingency?"

"I'm trying to remember," replied Paula slowly. "It's so long
ago. Ah, I've got it! I think it was after Bill died and Kitty knew
I was suspecting her. She asked what I would do if I really
believed she had killed him, and I said something about just
going out of her life for ever. What do you take this to mean,
James?"

"That she did kill him, I suppose."

"Yes. I think that too. And I've just remembered something
else she said. She said that I found it very difficult to live with
uncertainty. That was clever, considering that she didn't know
me very well."

"She was right," said James. "You do find it very difficult. She
must have liked you a lot, Paula."

"How so?"

"To send you this message. To remove your uncertainty and
set your mind at ease."

"You don't think it's meant to be mocking—sneering? She
was like that, you know."

"No. I don't think so. I think it's an act of kindness. I wonder what will become of her?"

James turned the postcard over to show the picture side.

"Liberty," said Paula. "She paid a high price for it. I believe it lost her the one man she loved."

ABOUT THE AUTHOR

Anna Clarke was born in Cape Town and educated in Montreal and Oxford. She holds degrees in both economics and English literature, and has held a variety of jobs, mostly in publishing and university administration. She is the author of twenty-two previously published suspense novels, including *Last Seen in London,* and *Soon She Must Die.* This is her sixth novel to feature Paula Glenning.